HOW TO START A
ROMANTIC
ENCOUNTER

WHERE TO GO TO FIND LOVE AND
WHAT TO SAY WHEN YOU FIND IT

LARRY GLANZ
ROBERT H. PHILLIPS

Avery Publishing Group
Garden City Park, New York

Cover Design: Ann Vestal
In-House Editors: Elaine Will Sparber and Marie Caratozzolo
Typesetter: Bonnie Freid
Printer: Paragon Press, Honesdale, Pennsylvania

Publisher's Cataloging-in-Publication Data

Glanz, Larry
   How to start a romantic encounter : where to go to find love and
what to say when you find it / Larry Glanz & Robert H. Phillips.
   p. cm.
   Includes index.
   ISBN 0-89529-580-6

   1. Dating (Social custom) 2. Single people—United States—Life
skills guides. 3. Interpersonal communication. 4. Mate selection.
I. Title.

HQ801.G53 1993   646.77
                                               QBI93-22067

10 9 8 7 6 5 4 3 2

Contents

Acknowledgments vii

Introduction 1

Part I Getting Started

1. Making the Most of Your Product 5

2. Developing a List of Prospects 15

3. Preparing to Meet Someone 23

4. Starting a Conversation 29

5. Following Up and Closing the Deal 41

6. Using Three Winning Techniques 57

7. Breaking the Ice with Attention Getters 63

Part II Making Contact

8. Choosing Contact Sites and Functions. 73

9. Singles Dances and Parties. 77

10. Entertainment Sites 87

11. Organizational Work. 93

12. Dining 99

13. Business and Professional Activities 107

14. Outdoor Activities 111

15. Trips 119

16. Sports 125

17. Hobbies and Self-Help. 133

18. Indoor Meeting Places. 147

19. Shopping 153

20. Transportation. 165

21. Singles Dating Clubs and Video Dating Services 173

22. Personal Ads 177

23. How to Meet Someone During the Holidays 185

A Bright New Beginning. 189

Index 193

To my mother,
to whom I owe it all.

To my dear departed dad,
whose spirit lives on within me.

To my sister, Barbara, and nieces, Wendy and Lisa,
who have been with me through troubled times.

Special thanks to my stepdad, Harry,
who has been an unbelievable help to me.

To my buddy Craig Berman,
who epitomizes what it means to be a friend.

L.G.

To my wife, Sharon, and my sons, Michael, Larry, and Steven,
who provide the nucleus.

To my parents and sister,
who provided the foundation.

To my late grandparents,
who provided the inspiration.

And to the rest of my family, in-laws, and friends,
who provide the icing on the cake.

R.H.P.

Acknowledgments

I would like to thank all the people I have met who have encouraged me to write this book.

Special thanks go out to Rick Berkowitz, Carol Cartaino, Eric Spinman, Judy of Earthlight, Shawn Dennehy, Kenny Smith, and others too numerous to mention for their valuable input.

Rudy Shur, my publisher, who helped mold my dream into a reality.

Dr. Robert Phillips, my co-author, who took my raw recruit of a manuscript and whipped it into a marine.

To editors Elaine Will Sparber and Marie Caratozzolo, publisher's assistant Beth Croteau, and the rest of the Avery staff.

And a very special thank you to the following people for their invaluable input into the making of this book: Jason Caratozzolo, Linda Comac, Bonnie Freid, Dave Grossnickle, Karen Hay, Harlan Krawitz, Steve Liebold, John Pospisil, Evan Schwartz, Justin Shur, and Shoshana Shur.

L.G.

In addition to the people mentioned above, I would like to thank the members of my staff—Melissa Sheinwold, Carmela Vecchio, Donna Storan, and Ann Dominger—who were instrumental in the prompt and efficient preparation of the drafts and final copy of this manuscript.

R.H.P.

Introduction

S uccess in attaining your goals in life begins with knowledge. Congratulations! By obtaining this book, you have taken an important step. You want to acquire the essential knowledge to help you reach a specific goal, namely, to meet and win the person you desire to spend your days, evenings, and possibly the rest of your life with.

In this book, we have taken a serious, practical, but lighthearted look at the "wheres" and "how tos" of locating and attracting someone special. It could be that incredible hunk of a guy living in the apartment upstairs, the goddess in the tight leotards at the fitness center, the handsome salesman who comes to your office to sell widgets, or the stunning brunette with the luscious lips and big eyes whose car pulls up next to yours at a red light.

The directions, techniques, and philosophies that follow have been tried time and time again with amazingly successful results. Read the book several times if necessary, until you feel comfortable enough to apply the knowledge that is suitable for your particular situation. Then use this new-found information to find that special someone.

Chances are you wouldn't be reading this book unless you felt you had a few weak points that could use some strengthening. You probably want to become adept at implementing at least some of the strategies found within this book's covers. Remember, it will take an open-minded attitude on your part to put your new knowledge to work.

Essentially, this book is for any man or woman who is seeking a relationship to enhance his or her life and end loneliness. It is for singles (of any age) who want to improve their confidence and skills when meeting people.

Going through life as a single person might make you feel lonely, depressed, sick, or frustrated. It may be especially difficult for you to watch couples that are happy. If you're fortunate enough to meet someone nice, but it doesn't evolve into the relationship you had hoped for, you may feel even further unhappiness.

The singles scene today can be *scary!* We want to help you enjoy it and meet some wonderful people in the process. So how do you go about joining the couples scene? Read on.

Part I
Getting Started

1. Making the Most
of Your Product

Girls, have you ever walked though a shopping mall or gone out to dinner with friends and spotted a handsome, well-dressed man who was with a woman with below-average looks? Haven't you wondered what she has that helped her find such a man? You may have thought, "She must work for him, because he could do so much better—*me!*"

Guys, when at a sporting event or a dance club, have you ever noticed an absolute knock-out of a woman with a wimpy or nerdy man? Haven't you asked yourself, "What does he have that enabled him to find such a beauty? He must be rich because there is no way on earth that she could be interested in a guy like him, not when *I'm* available."

Well, beauty is indeed in the eye of the beholder. But if these thoughts perplex you, then you might want to begin by taking stock of your own strengths and weaknesses. Ask yourself:

What type of appearance do I make? How do others perceive me? Do I have stylish clothes? Am I clean and well groomed? Am I a nice person all of the time? Do I really believe I am capable of meeting someone who wants me and will accept me with whatever faults that I have? Is it really worth putting forth the effort to improve myself in order to meet someone nice? How badly do I want someone special in my life? Am I reading this book out of curiosity or do I really mean business?

Take stock of who you are. List your strong points (don't be modest, now) as well as your weak points (be constructive). Identify those areas that you'd like to improve and then start doing it! Some of the most common areas targeted for self-improvement revolve around appearance, manners, habits, and attitude. Let's discuss some of these areas in more detail.

MAXIMIZE YOUR APPEARANCE

Each person is born with particular looks. Some people are fortunate enough to be really good-looking. Others may not be as fortunate and may have to work harder to maximize their best features.

Making the most of the looks you are born with is a lot like playing gin rummy. You can improve the hand you're dealt by selecting other cards. If you make the correct selections, you can win the game. The same principle applies to your appearance. If you put forth enough effort, you can improve upon the looks you are born with. This can result in increased success in finding that someone special and winning at the age-old game of love.

Think of yourself as a product. Now, how marketable are you? Do you have good attention-getting packaging? Does this packaging reflect who you really are? Does it present you in the best possible way? If the answer to any of these questions is no, or you're not sure, then you have found an area that needs improvement! You, in essence, must make yourself as salable and desirable as possible to potential prospects.

Okay, so you can't judge a book by its cover. But let's face it, the cover has to be sufficiently interesting in order for someone to want to open the book in the first place! If you're single and searching for a mate but convey a lackluster appearance, then you'll certainly want to start by concentrating your efforts on whipping your appearance into its most marketable shape.

Dressing for success is a key factor in practically all facets of life. Do you want to be successful in your efforts to meet someone? Then clean, well-kept, stylish clothes and shoes are a must. When was the last time you upgraded your wardrobe? Check it out now and make the necessary changes.

First impressions are critically important. Your appearance can be the difference when making contact with someone. No matter how bright, clever, entertaining, warm, talented, or delightful you are, few people will bother to notice these attributes if your exterior doesn't motivate them to stick around and discover it all.

So take stock. And be brutally honest. Which areas of your physical appearance could use some improvement? Consider your skin, smile, teeth, eyes, hair—all the areas that can give either an inviting or discouraging first impression. You may not always detect problems in these areas, but, rest assured, your prospects will!

The experts agree: Make the most of your physical features. It should be the first phase of your self-promotion campaign.

POLISH YOUR TABLE MANNERS

Table manners count, too. This is an area in which many people didn't receive proper guidance as children. Subsequently, they have grown into adults without a clue as to how to eat. Can poor manners be a turnoff? You bet your utensils they can! Which poor table manners are offensive? Speaking while you have food in your mouth, smacking your lips, slurping, neglecting excess food on your face or teeth, or holding utensils like a shovel are just a few unappetizing examples of offensive table manners.

You may look "mahvelous," but crummy table manners can kill those good looks. If you're not sure whether or not your manners are up to snuff, seek out a book on proper etiquette at the library, consult a professional, or ask someone whom you trust and know will be honest.

Remember, the singles dating scene often involves dining in restaurants. So this part of your act is crucial to your success.

ELIMINATE BAD HABITS

There are many bad habits that can doom a new relationship. No, we're not talking just of addictions to drugs or alcohol (which can certainly doom you, too). There are other addictions or habits that can have a negative impact on your efforts, as well.

Smoking

Do you smoke cigarettes, cigars, or pipes? If the answer is yes, it might be smart to refrain from smoking in the presence of a nonsmoker. As many nonsmokers simply refuse to date smokers, exercising control of this habit could expand your list of dating prospects. Better yet, this willpower could give you the courage and motivation to quit smoking altogether! The benefits? You will eliminate the offensive smell of smoke on your breath, hair, and clothing; add years to your life; and save a substantial amount of money on tobacco products and possibly medical bills!

Yawning

Yawning gives the distinct impression that you are either bored, disinterested, or tired. You don't want to be thought of this way, do you? No one wants to be on a date with someone who appears physically exhausted and in need of sleep.

Some people, merely out of habit, have a tendency to yawn even when they are not tired. If you are one of these people, make a conscious effort to keep from performing this "act of boredom" when you're out with someone. This mental awareness will help you to control your habit. At the very least, you should try to cover up the yawn or make it less noticeable.

If you yawn because you are truly in need of some sleep, then it is probably best to call it a night and get to bed. But for any future dates or plans you might have, be sure you're well rested the night before. The day of the date, try to catch some zzz's after work or school to recharge your body. Remember, a well-rested, enthusiastic person is a fun person to be with.

Staring

Staring is another habit that can certainly frighten away prospects. It can be too intense and make others wary of you. Furthermore, if you're on a date, staring at someone else can be a supreme insult to the person you're with. When you're in the company of someone you like or to whom you are attracted, always give 100 percent of your attention to this person. Make eye contact with your date. Undivided attention will help generate chemistry between the two of you.

Other Bad Habits

Do you use foul language, bite your fingernails, or crack your knuckles? These are not positive attributes, and they can be detrimental in attracting prospective partners. What can you do about these and other bad habits? Begin by making a list of these negative attributes (don't be embarrassed—you're helping yourself achieve a goal!), then put the list in a prominent place where you can review it often. Monitor your progress in controlling or eliminating these habits. All it takes is a dedicated, conscientious effort on your part to get yourself on the right track. Once you have all or most of these negative habits under control, not only will you be a better person for your efforts, but you will increase the likelihood of success in meeting someone special.

IMPROVE YOUR ATTITUDE

Now that you've started to work on your physical appearance and behavior, it's time to go to work on your mental frame of mind. Getting your mental attitude synchronized with your physical being is very important. In fact, a positive attitude can make all the difference in insuring success.

If you are absolutely serious about your mission, you must always maintain a positive frame of mind. For your effort and commitment, hopefully, you will be rewarded with true love. Sure, it can be very depressing, frustrating, and expensive to pursue opportunities to meet someone special. Nevertheless, the end result of finding that someone and ending your loneliness is well worth whatever effort is required.

Keep the following thoughts in mind:

- You really want someone in your life *now*, not sometime in the next ten years.

- That special someone is out there waiting to meet you.

- That person can become attracted to you.

- It is worth putting forth any effort to meet that special person.

In addition to keeping these thoughts in mind, your attitude may need some fine-tuning. Are you a nice person all the time? Do you ever act like you woke up and had a bowl of tacks for breakfast? It is a very important part of your self-promotion program to make a conscious effort to be the nicest person you can possibly be. Be caring, polite, respectful, and thoughtful at all times. Treat others the way you would want to be treated, but don't expect anything in return.

Rid yourself of any hostility, anger, or belligerence that may have resulted from previous bad relationships or marriages. Remember: The next person you meet is *not* responsible for the "tortures" of your past. While you may have every right to be angry or bitter, do you have the right to transfer these feelings to a new person? Of course not. And remember, this new person may be just what you need to be happy again.

A hostile attitude can be a real turnoff to a potential prospect. Anyone with common sense will avoid you like the plague the moment your negative attitude surfaces. Of course, professional counseling can help you resolve hostilities and other mental attitude problems. Go with the odds. It is more likely that someone special will discover and fall in love with a genuinely nice, positive-thinking person than a negatively charged one.

BE FLEXIBLE

Are you willing to change your ways or behavior patterns? As you get older, you may become more set in your ways, making you less flexible than you once were. It is always important to be flexible in your thinking. Be willing to make compromises. The person you desire may have firm unyielding beliefs in a particular area, and your ability to "go with the flow" may help make a relationship possible.

The following example illustrates how the ability to be flexible can enhance an existing relationship. Joe was a classic rock-and-roll junkie, while Mary enjoyed country music. That was fine when they listened to their own radios, but when they were together, they compromised on jazz and soft rock. Every now and then, together they would listen to rock-and-roll or country music. Guess what? Joe found that he actually started to like some of the songs Mary liked, and vice versa. Fortunately, they were both flexible and willing to compromise. That's the key.

This same example of flexibility can encompass many different areas—foods, movies, sports, hobbies, and so on. It is an important ingredient in a successful relationship.

CHANNEL YOUR WILLPOWER

Let's review. Can you honestly say your attitude is good? Your disposition in control? Your less-attractive habits in check? Your appearance better than ever? Great. Now it's time to address the next item—willpower. This is the time to face your greatest inner strength. It's the time to exercise your power to "stick to it" until you find success. If you give up on your goal, the odds of meeting the right someone will be reduced.

This book advocates an active but low-key approach to meeting and attracting a potential partner. Chance is not enough. Not only do you need to develop the willpower to improve all aspects of your personal being, but you have to learn how to apply your knowledge.

Remember, your main source of strength is your inner self. How much do you want to improve your life? Dig down into that inner strength and make it happen. You have the willpower to find success!

SPEAK UP

As human beings, we are as unique as snowflakes. Each person reacts differently in social situations. And from these encounters different positive and negative feelings develop.

It is the ability to verbally communicate your innermost thoughts and feelings that helps you effectively create and advance interpersonal relationships in a positive manner. But what if your thoughts and feelings are directed inward instead of out toward the other person? Unfortunately, you're not doing much to enhance the future of the relationship. In addition, medical studies have found that people who hold back their feelings and keep them bottled up are at an increased risk for many debilitating illnesses.

Strive to be open and honest with the feelings you have in your heart and mind, and express them through words and actions. Through this communication, you can create a more solid bond with your prospect, gain more respect and loyalty for your honesty and openness, and maintain a healthier physical and emotional state.

BE ENCOURAGED . . . NOT DISCOURAGED

Accept the fact that not every potential prospect will be attracted to you or respond to you in a positive way. There has to be some interest on the other person's part. Do your best to be friendly, polite, and sincere. Try to apply the wisdom of this book in your attempt to cultivate interest in the other person. But keep in mind that the other person has likes and dislikes of his or her own.

The techniques in this book won't work with every person you encounter, and some rejection is a natural part of the process. But it is important to realize that people are not really rejecting you (they don't even know you, do they?). They're rejecting what they think they know. It's their loss. It is important for you to accept a rejection gracefully without becoming hostile or feeling hurt.

How do you know when to continue pursuing a prospect? Look for such signs as eye contact, a smile, positive body language (a lean in your direction, or an open, facing stance), or any effort that a potential prospect makes to communicate with you. If these signals stop or don't exist, chances are there may be no current interest on the prospect's part. You then have to decide whether to continue your pursuit or to move on to someone new.

Remember, any time you encounter a person who is not interested in you, tell yourself that there are plenty of others who will be interested once they get to know you. Do not become discouraged and do not let your attitude sour. Keep working at it—the results are worth it!

2. Developing a List of Prospects

*T*he information in this chapter will help you develop a list that includes people with whom you might be interested in having a romantic encounter. This list will include all prospects you frequently or infrequently come in contact with. As a single person, you should be aware of all potential prospects.

Basically, there are two categories of prospects—ones you will, in all probability, meet only once, and others whom you will encounter a number of times. For the "one-shot" encounters, you'll need to quickly break the ice, get a conversation started, then "close the deal." In this type of situation, remember that you'll probably have one opportunity only. It may be your "only chance to dance."

For the sake of this chapter, we'll be discussing only those prospects you're likely to see more than one time. This might include people who work in stores you frequent, neighbors, close friends of family members, classmates, or work acquaintances to name a few.

Your key to developing a successful list is to always remember your prospects' names, as well as any significant information about them. Any time you meet a prospective love interest, immediately jot down his or her name along with when, how, and where you met. List any observations (be a sharp detective) and include even seemingly insignificant details that you can recall from the encounter. Record this data on a card or notepad that you keep in your wallet or pocketbook.

In the sales field, this technique is called "prospecting." Potential new accounts or customer leads are logged onto account-information cards where prospects' names and pertinent information are stored. The wealth of information that is accumulated on these cards helps people in the sales field convert leads into accounts or customers. It helps salespeople hone in on a prospect's "hot buttons." These buttons must first be targeted, then pushed in order for the sale to be made. A salesperson's success rate is reliant upon how skilled he or she is at identifying these buttons.

The information on your cards should help you convert prospects into dates and, hopefully, arrive at that successful relationship. Use this information to target your prospect's hot buttons.

It's a good idea to periodically review your list. The next time you encounter one of your prospects (whether by chance or through "planning"), you will be able to remember the person's name and a few bits of pertinent information about them. This knowledge can be a welcome icebreaker during an encounter.

PUTTING THEORY INTO PRACTICE

How can your prospect list help you? To illustrate, let's take a look at Sue's list:

Tom— Works at stationery store, Lakers fan, met on Saturday afternoon at 2:30.

Jack— Neighbor in adjoining apartment complex, fireman, has German Shepherd named "Brutus," met on Tuesday night at 10:30 while he was walking dog.

Bill— Met on Monday morning at 9:00 at local 7–11 (he was getting coffee), owns construction company.

Now, let's see how Sue used the information on her list to press one of Tom's hot buttons. Sue wasn't really a sports fan, let alone a basketball fan, but the first time she met Tom she figured that he liked the Los Angeles Lakers because he was wearing a Lakers cap. So, for the entire next week, she scanned the sports pages to see how the Lakers were doing. It just so happened that on Thursday night of that week, the Lakers won a double-overtime thriller against the New York Knicks on a last-second buzzer beater. Armed with this information, Sue went to the stationery store about 2:30 the following Saturday afternoon, "prospecting" for Tom under the guise of seeking stationery supplies. Their conversation went like this:

Sue: Hi, Tom. How've you been?

Tom: Oh, I'm fine.

Sue: You should be more than fine. You should be in heaven after that double-overtime Lakers win over the Knicks on Thursday.

Tom: That was such a great game! I'm sorry, I forgot your name.

Sue: Sue.

Tom: I'm not very good with names. Are you a Lakers fan, Sue?

Sue: I'm starting to become one.

Tom: A Lakers game is an experience for me. I'm a diehard fan.

Sue: I've never been to a Lakers game, but I'd love to go to one.

Tom: Well, if you'd like, maybe I could take you to one.

Sue: That would be nice.

Tom: I have to get back to work here. Why don't you give me your number so I can call you to make plans. I'll check my Lakers schedule when I get home.

This example shows the importance of keeping prospect information. Sue knew the day and time Tom was likely to be working. She was prepared to speak with Tom about the Lakers, which was one of his hot buttons.

There is an old saying, "He who fails to plan, plans to fail." Sue put considerable planning and preparation into developing her prospect Tom. And that is what moved the odds for success in her favor. If Sue had not remembered or taken note of Tom's name and his interest in the Lakers, he might not have taken the time to make small talk with her. But because Sue was prepared, she caught Tom off guard and commanded his attention and interest.

Knowing even a little information about a prospect will help you make a connection. Simply remembering the name and anything significant about the person will garner immediate attention.

Interested in another example? Let's take a look at John's list:

Mandy—Lottery-ticket cashier at drugstore, loves jazz, met on Wednesday night, works Tuesday through Friday from 5:00 to 8:00 p.m.

Alice—Receptionist in dentist's office, divorced, loves to ski, has six-year-old daughter and four-year-old son.

April—In political science class, wants to be an attorney, loves horses, going to Aruba over winter break.

John really wanted to develop a relationship with April. As they were college classmates, he was able to easily discover a few bits of information about her. When he ran into her during registration for the following semester, he was confident enough to approach her and begin a conversation. The information he had gathered helped him break the ice. Their conversation went like this:

John: Hi, April. How was Aruba?

April: Oh, it was great. My friends and I had a wonderful time. I'm sorry, but I forgot your name.

John: It's John. We were in Dr. Wilson's political science class last semester.

April: Oh, that's right. I remember.

John: You have a great tan.

April: Actually, I *had* a great tan, but it's starting to fade now. My girlfriends and I spent most of our days on the beach. It was so relaxing.

John: Did you happen to go horseback riding on the beach while you were there?

April: No, but I'm sure I would've loved it. I can't believe you remembered that I like horseback riding.

John: April, I remember most things about nice people.

April: Oh, that's so sweet.

John: Do you ride horses in the winter?

April: Not really. It's usually too cold for me.

John: What do you enjoy doing during the winter?

April: I guess I like to go to the movies and out to eat.

John: Me, too. And if that's an invitation, I immediately accept!

April: (*Laughs*) You're funny, John.

John: Feed me and entertain me, and I'm a happy camper.

April: (*Laughs again*) Have you seen any good movies lately?

John: I was so busy with holiday parties and family get-togethers over winter break that I didn't have a chance to see any movies. Are there any good ones out there?

April: Oh, yes. Actually there are a couple of movies that look pretty interesting.

John: Want to join me for dinner and a movie this weekend? It would certainly be the highlight of my semester.

April: I think that would be nice.

John: Great! Let me have your phone number, and I'll call you later so we can make definite plans.

April: Okay, it's 555-5045. If I'm not home, leave a message on my machine. As a matter of fact, let me have your number in case you can't reach me.

In this example, John's list provided him with the right ammunition to press a few of April's hot buttons. Most of the conversation was centered around April's interests, and John was clever enough to pepper their chat with a few compliments and some humor. Also, he was able to connect with her on common ground (dinner and movies). Although John was a little aggressive, his use of humor and sincerity helped him create a subtle urgency with April in terms of when they'd be speaking again to make plans for their date.

If you put the same amount of effort and preparation into developing your prospect list as you do with other priorities in your life, you'll find that this list will yield a gold mine of opportunities for you. These opportunities will lead you to dates and, hopefully, fulfilling relationships.

QUALIFYING YOUR PROSPECTS

It's important for you to be aware of the qualities you desire in another person. An excellent way for you to develop this framework is by preparing a list of your requirements. If your prospects fall within this list, you know you'll be spending quality time with people who interest you. In the sales field, this is called "qualifying the prospect." And it helps to determine which prospects have the strongest potential to become a sale.

What's the most effective way of qualifying a prospect? By asking questions and being a good attentive listener. A good listener is one who maintains eye contact with the speaker, does not interrupt, and stays focused on the answers.

Ask thought-provoking questions that involve more than just a yes or no response. This shows you are genuinely interested in the other person. At the same time, the responses will give you a splendid idea as to whether or not the prospect meets your qualifications. Also, if you are shy, quiet, or a poor conversationalist, asking questions will help take the pressure to speak off of your shoulders.

Know your absolute, non-negotiable requirements for potential prospects. Does your dream mate have to have dark hair? Light hair? Or does it matter? What about height and weight? Does the prospect have to have a good physique? Must this person be of a particular religion? Be careful not to be overly critical when listing your requirements. Try to be realistic in your expectations. Don't allow the slightest flaw or weakness to eliminate a potential prospect.

There are some requirements in prospective dates that you may genuinely feel are non-negotiable. For example, you may be a nonsmoker who doesn't want to be around a smoker, or maybe you're a college graduate and wish to date only college-educated individuals. These are non-negotiable requirements. You may be of a certain religion and don't want to become involved with anyone outside of that religion.

Does it matter to you if a prospect has been married before and has children? Although some people may find this situation okay, others may find it unacceptable. A parent may put his or her children first, before you. If this does not suit you, then date only people who are single or divorced with no children, and make this one of your non-negotiable requirements.

A WORD TO THE WISE

Qualifying your prospects is important when seeking out someone special. Be careful, however, not to over-qualify a potential prospect. Try not to act like a Gestapo commandante who is interrogating a prisoner. And don't appear to be one step away from demanding a urine specimen and stool sample! In other words, don't be overly critical in your demands. If you are, most of your potential prospects will be disqualified for one reason or another.

Know that you will always find something not to like about another person. But ask yourself, is it enough to eliminate the prospect? Try to seek out the good qualities of that person and do your best to overlook minimal imperfections.

3. Preparing to
Meet Someone

*T*here are two main, incredibly simple steps to meeting someone. Well, let's rephrase that. The steps themselves are simple, but knowing how to put them into practice, ah, that can be more difficult. (But then again, that's what the rest of this book is about.)

The first step to meeting someone is being in the right place at the right time. Of course, this meeting doesn't necessarily have to happen by chance or coincidentally. If you see an attractive prospect, it shouldn't matter where you are. You are in the right place and it is the right time! Of course, luck and fate certainly play a role, but you have to help yourself along. You have the power. Just do things. Get out there. Go where single prospects are likely to be found.

Once you find yourself in the right place at the right time, it is time for step two—doing something constructive in order to meet that person. When you find yourself in a situation in which an encounter is likely to occur, it's up to you to take the necessary action to make contact with that prospect. Naturally, there are different approaches for different situations. There are scores of creative icebreakers at your disposal. These icebreakers are designed to help you make the initial contact with a person, as well as, hopefully, elicit a positive response.

The balance of this book covers in detail the specific "wheres" and "how tos" for meeting others. (Learning the elements of good conversation, knowing the best meeting places, and familiarizing yourself with lines for breaking the ice are discussed at length.) First, however, an important concept needs to be discussed—increasing your odds for success.

INCREASING THE ODDS

As a single person who is interested in meeting other singles, you should constantly strive to stack all possible odds in your favor. In the previous chapters we have discussed the best ways for you to "package" yourself for the most effective presentation. We have also pointed out important considerations when seeking prospective love-interest selections.

Now that you know how to look your best, and you have a good idea of what to look for in a prospect, how can you increase the likelihood of meeting others? Through two general techniques—playing the numbers game and being on a twenty-four-hour-a-day alert.

Playing the Numbers Game

Playing the numbers game is a technique that incorporates the concept of networking. When you network, you use everyone you know and interact with to introduce you to or "fix you up" with other single people.

Playing the numbers game increases your odds of meeting eligible prospects. Basically, you should be ready, willing, and able to seize every opportunity to meet new people. The more people you meet, the better your chances are of finding that special someone.

Sources to tap for networking are family members, friends, neighbors, business associates, and virtually anyone else you know. It is not a disgrace to let someone know you are single and interested in meeting the right person. "If you know someone nice, I would like to meet them," is all you need to say in order to get the ball rolling. If you are genuinely sincere, people will hear you and try to help. Haven't you noticed that everyone seems to know someone they would like to introduce to another person?

It's important for you to meet as many prospects as you can. It is equally as important to be polite to every person that you meet. Even if a meeting doesn't lead to romance, it might evolve into a good friendship. And who knows, he or she may be just the person who introduces you to that special someone.

Be sure to thank the person who set up your introduction, even if things don't work out. In addition to being the polite thing to do, it will keep the door open for future introductions through this person.

The more ways you try to connect with interesting prospects, the greater your chances are of meeting the right person. You'll have the power of numbers in your favor. There is an old saying among salespeople, "Throw enough garbage against the wall and a certain amount is going to stick." Just as in sales, you may have to meet hundreds of potential prospects before you meet the one person who is truly suitable for you.

So play the numbers game. Be prepared and committed to networking. It can help you change a less-than-desirable social life into one that gives you satisfaction and fulfillment.

Twenty-Four-Hour-a-Day Alert

The philosophy of this book is to at all times be physically, mentally, and emotionally prepared to attract and meet a potential love interest. It means always having a pen within your reach to receive or to give a telephone number. If a piece of paper (or matchbook cover or cocktail napkin) is not available, it means you have to be willing to have a telephone number temporarily written on your hand, arm, knee, or whatever bodily appendage is readily (and appropriately) accessible! This willingness will undoubtedly demonstrate to your prospect an immediate desire and enthusiasm on your part, which will score points for you.

Being on a twenty-four-hour-a-day alert means looking attractive, acting upbeat, and being prepared to meet a potential prospect at any time. This means when you're walking your dog (whether it's 10:30 at night or 6:00 in the morning), running out to the convenience store for a quart of milk, or taking a walk to the corner mailbox. In other words, you should feel confident enough in your appearance to be ready to meet potential prospects anytime and anywhere. If you don't, you'll be doing yourself a great disservice. Don't think it's enough to be armed and ready only for singles events!

For example, what happens when you see someone attractive who makes your heart pound incessantly and gives you goose bumps from your nose to your toes? If you don't feel confident enough in the way you look, you will probably let the opportunity to meet that person slip away. Your dream mate will drive off into the sunset and you'll want to drive off a cliff out of frustration. Surely you can think of at least one time in your life when you wished you had made contact with someone you were attracted to. Didn't you feel a little disappointed in yourself for letting the opportunity pass you by?

By the way, if you're a woman, we're not suggesting that you spend an hour putting on make-up before you go out for that quart of milk. Nor do we recommend that a man spends time shaving before he goes out to walk the dog. Do the best you can, within reason, to make yourself neat and appealing. It's worth the extra few minutes at home grooming yourself before stepping outside. This little extra effort spent on your appearance will give you an extra edge of confidence, which just may help you meet the love of your life—the one you won't let get away.

SUMMING IT UP

When searching for that special someone, always remember the importance of stacking the odds in your favor. Utilize the networking technique, which enables you to come into contact with large numbers of eligible prospects. And always be "on alert" to seize any opportunity that comes your way.

4. Starting a
Conversation

Some people are able to talk easily and naturally in any situation. Others seem to get tongue-tied whenever they open their mouths (except when they're eating!). Unless you have eyes that speak for you, you're going to need some conversation skills to help you break the ice during your first encounter with a prospect. Good skills in this area also enable you to keep the interaction going once the conversation has begun.

Breaking the ice is very difficult for some people. If you are one who falls into this category, you must be able to do or say something to break the tension and elicit a response of some sort. The main purpose of breaking the ice is to get the prospect to start talking, for any reason. Let's say that you feel a strong attraction to someone. Along with this attraction, you may also experience some nervousness or anxiety in initiating verbal contact. You may feel intense pressure to say the right thing. The fear of rejection may also be on your mind, complicating your dilemma even further. Additionally, your brain may remind you that the person you want to approach is a complete stranger—what is this person going to think of you? How is he or she going to respond to your approach? All of these insecurities can cause you to feel anxious and uncomfortable about initiating that first contact.

So, how do you get things started? How can you rid yourself of these anxieties and feel confident enough to break the ice? Read on.

YOUR ATTITUDE

Before you approach your prospect, get yourself into a helpful state of mind. When you make that initial contact, be sure to maintain a light, carefree "what-the-heck" attitude. If your icebreaker leads to conversation, act interested and sincere, but don't be intense or offensive.

Also, keep in mind that your first contact with another person doesn't necessarily have to be a verbal one. Be creative in your approach. Do whatever it takes, within reason, to get that person to notice you. For example, in bars and dance clubs it is acceptable to have a bartender or waitress deliver a drink with your compliments to someone you're admiring. This tactic is sure to get you noticed, and you never know what might develop after that. We know of a certain gentleman who employs a creative variation on this approach. When he is out having breakfast, he has the waitress bring a glass of freshly squeezed orange juice along with a short pleasant note to someone he finds attractive. He continually meets and dates attractive women this way. (See Chapter 7 for more nonverbal attention getters.)

BOUNCING BACK

Know that many individuals who have become skilled at meeting other people may not have always been so successful. More than likely, they have experienced failure in at least some of their attempts. However, let's not use the word "failure." Rather, let's say that they haven't always succeeded. Practice, diligence, and the ability to bounce back helped them sharpen their confrontational skills.

You (like everyone else) will experience setbacks from time to time. Don't be discouraged by "non-successes." No matter how many times you don't succeed, always remember that it takes only one victory to land your true love.

BREAKING THE ICE

Let's assume that you're ready. You've packaged yourself to the max, you're in the right place at the right time, and you see someone who interests you. So what do you do now? Well, you can't wait for your prospect to make the first move (although it sure would be nice, wouldn't it?). You've got to begin the conversation yourself.

This is probably one of the hardest phases of meeting someone, especially if you are shy. Generally, it's much easier to answer someone else's question than it is to pose one of your own. But what if your prospect doesn't make the first move? Are you willing to let that person slip away? What can you say (with a minimal amount of trembling) to start things off?

Your initial contact should begin with a one-liner to break the ice—either a question or statement. Your question may be funny, designed to get the person to giggle, or it might be more serious, intended to elicit a thought-out response. Your statement might be an opinion that you expect the person to agree or even disagree with, or a comment that you hope will be met with an interested reply.

Rehearse, Rehearse, Rehearse

As you read the various icebreakers that follow, you may come across several that you like. You might, however, think you'll sound foolish if you actually tried to use one. Not to worry! All you have to do is practice saying the lines aloud when you're alone. When it's time for the actual line delivery, you'll sound smooth, confident, and natural. Rehearsing is the key.

Throughout this chapter, as well as Part II, scores of icebreaking lines are presented. Whenever you come across one that fits your personality, check it. Feel free to use these lines exactly as they are written, modify them to fit your personal style, or use them as a springboard to create lines of your own. The list is limitless.

Start out by selecting a few icebreakers, and practice saying them out loud while standing in front of a mirror. Get used to the way they sound. Try delivering the lines to a family member or friend and gauge the reaction. After all, if a line is stupid, do you really want to use it? On the other hand, if your "audience" likes what you're saying and the confident manner of your delivery, you'll probably feel more comfortable trying that line on a prospect. Practicing will help you rid yourself of anxiety. In a while, your line delivery will be so natural that your icebreakers won't be confused with come-ons.

Keep a list of your favorite icebreakers in a handy place, such as your wallet or pocketbook. If you feel it is necessary, quickly review the list right before you approach your prospect. Then go for it! When you find yourself in the right place at the right time, use an appropriate icebreaker to help you make contact and get the ball rolling.

TRIED-AND-TRUE ICEBREAKING LINES

The following list includes some of the simplest things to say to another person to initiate contact and generate conversation. Realize that these lines by themselves won't establish a long-term relationship, but they can get another person to notice you and respond to what you have said.

Different lines are better suited for different personalities. No one will feel truly comfortable with all of the lines found in this book. Select only those that you feel most at ease with. Keep in mind that the success of these lines largely depends on your delivery. Creative lines may require effective voice inflections, facial expressions, or body mannerisms. (All of which you will develop through experience.) Above all, use only those lines that feel right to you, ones that most closely reflect your personality.

With any of the following lines, approach your prospect, establish eye contact, and confidently say:

☐ "Hi, my name is ____. What's yours?"

☐ "Hi, what's your name? Mine's ____."

☐ "Excuse me, do I know you from somewhere?"
(*This is one of the oldest yet most effective lines used. However, you must sound sincere or the line will come off as a come-on!*)

☐ "Do you come here often?"

☐ "What do you think of this place?"

☐ "What have you heard about this place?"

☐ "Some weather, isn't it?"

☐ "This place is really nice, isn't it?"

☐ "Have you ever been here before?"

☐ "Do you live around here?"

☐ "Gee, I'm sorry. Did I bump into you?"

☐ "Can I help you with that?"

☐ "Here, let me get that for you."

☐ "Excuse me, do you have the time?"

☐ "Have I met you before? You look so familiar."

☐ "May I ask you a question?"
(*Make sure you have a good question or two to ask when the prospect says yes.*)

☐ "Do you mind my telling you how good you look in that ___?"
(*Insert appropriate article of clothing.*)

☐ "Will you forgive me for saying that you look great in that color? It really brings out the beauty of your eyes/skin/hair."

☐ "Do you mind my telling you that you remind me of my ___?"
(*Insert name of friend, relative, or acquaintance.*)

☐ "You look like someone I know I would want to meet."

☐ "I wish I had the perfect line to get you to start talking to me, but I don't. So how about if I just say, 'Hi, my name is ___'?"

OTHER ICEBREAKING LINES

The icebreaking lines just presented are very basic. Sometimes, however, you may be in a more humorous or playful mood, or the situation may call for a more imaginative icebreaker. Many of the following lines may sound slightly unusual, but one may be just perfect for that nonbasic moment.

Some people may find it difficult to deliver a basic line, let alone one that is out of the ordinary. An icebreaker with a light touch, though, can be more fun. And no matter what you say, remember that the icebreaker's goal is to open the door to conversation.

Because of this, even a negative response from your prospect is better than no response at all. You can always follow up on the negative reaction with a comment such as, "Well, I guess that was a pretty stupid thing to say, but I wasn't sure of the best way to come over and say hello. Do you forgive me?" or "Okay, I'll admit that that was a corny line, but I really just wanted to talk to you." Such follow-up lines often smooth ruffled feathers and neutralize initial negative reactions.

As with the tried-and-true icebreakers, some of the following lines will roll off your tongue, while others will catch in your throat. Read through the lines and check those that best fit your personal style. Practice saying the lines to yourself in the mirror, to your dog, and to attractive characters on the television screen. Again, when ready to use a line, approach your prospect and establish eye contact first.

- ☐ "I hope the rest of my day looks as good as you do."
- ☐ "Excuse me, but how does someone become a member of your fan club?"
- ☐ "The moment I saw you, I knew I wanted to be your friend."
- ☐ "You look incredible. May I have a picture of you to put on my refrigerator door?"
- ☐ "You're the type of person I've always fantasized about."
- ☐ "I would follow you anywhere."
- ☐ "I feel thoroughly enriched after seeing you."
- ☐ "You look like a million bucks after taxes."
- ☐ "I'd love to hold hands with you. My fingers would be ecstatic."
- ☐ "I think I'm falling in like with you."
- ☐ "You have pretty eyes. Are they real?"
  (*To be said with obvious humor.*)

☐ "Do you have a quarter? My mom told me to call her when I found the girl/guy of my dreams."

☐ "Do you know anyone who is exactly like you in every way but isn't currently involved with someone?"

☐ "If I had to, I'd get a second job just to be with you on a first date."

☐ "I'm touched by this chance encounter with you. Would you care to honor this special occasion and join me for some cookies and milk?"

☐ "I have to get to know you."

☐ "Gee, your hair smells terrific."

☐ "You look good enough to be on a picture postcard."

☐ "On a scale of one to ten, you break the scales in a good way."

☐ "One look at you and it's impossible to ignore you."

☐ "I can't let you walk by without at least opening the door for you."

☐ "I don't think I could ever get tired of looking at you."

☐ "You're definitely worth a second glance."

☐ "When you meet someone new, you can be either honest or phony. All I can do with you is speak from my heart."

☐ "I just bought this book and I'd like to try one of the icebreaking lines in order to meet you. I really want it to work, so would you tell me what you think?"
(*Use this line anywhere and on anyone. Simply show the book to your prospect, then watch that person immediately smile or break into a good-natured laugh. This line works like a charm because it disarms the prospect with a laugh or a smile, yet it lets them know you are sincere in your effort to meet them. This may be one of the best icebreaking lines of all.*)

Any of the icebreaking lines (or modifications of these lines) can be starters in your attempt to meet people. And be aware that they are exactly that—starters. Although it can happen, please realize that it usually takes more than an icebreaker to get a conversation flowing. Always arm yourself with a few follow-up lines that you can use in response to a prospect's reaction to your initial icebreaker. Keep some appropriate comments, questions, or other icebreakers up your sleeve. Remember, even a creative icebreaker can meet with a dead-end reaction, and you must always be ready to meet such reactions head-on.

To further illustrate this point, let's say, for example, you are at a dance club and see someone you'd like to meet. You walk over and initiate contact with this person by using an icebreaker:

You: Excuse me, do you have the time?

Prospect: 9:30.

Okay, now what? You've broken the ice and made initial contact, but what next? You must be ready with another line:

You: Do you think you could give me the next five minutes?

Prospect: Well, uh, I guess so.

Here's another dead end. Looks like you have to work a little harder:

You: Is this the first time you've been here? I don't remember seeing you here before.

Prospect: Yes, it is. A couple of my friends came here last week and they really loved it. I can see why. The decor is great and . . .

Well, congratulations! It took a little more than a simple

icebreaker to get a dialogue going, but you hung in there and did it.

Let's take a look at another hypothetical situation in which the importance of knowing how to follow-up an icebreaker is illustrated. You find yourself in the same dance club:

You: This place is really nice, isn't it?

Prospect: Yes, it is.

Here's that old familiar dead end, but you're going to face it head on with a little humor:

You: So, do you think this is the spot where they found the body? (*Pause*) Just kidding.

Prospect: (*Laughs*) Cute.

Once again, being armed and prepared helped you pave the way for a conversation.

You want one more dance-club scenario? Okay then, here goes:

You: Excuse me, but how does one become a member of your fan club?

Prospect: (*Mildly annoyed*) Excuse me?

You: I just wanted to know how to join your fan club.

Prospect: (*More annoyed*) You can't.

Now there's a dead end if ever there was one. You may simply decide to lick your wounded ego and walk away before more damage is done. On the other hand, if you're adventurous, you might choose to give it one more shot:

You: Look, I know that was a really corny line. I guess

I just didn't know how to meet you. All I wanted to do was say hello.

Prospect: Well, at least that's a little more direct. I don't think I've seen you here before. . . .

Okay, so we've given this last scene somewhat of a happy ending. Of course, the prospect just as easily could have turned his or her back on your final attempt. And that is certainly something you should be prepared for. Just remember not to take a negative reaction personally. You can't expect each and every person to be receptive to your attempts at conversation. Learn from these experiences.

Once again, the important thing is to be prepared with more than just the simple icebreaker when you approach someone. Always have a few good follow-ups to help get that conversation off the ground. Detailed information on possible responses to your icebreakers and how to effectively follow them up is presented in Chapter 5.

In Part II, you'll find many more unusual, creative icebreakers. Some of these lines are statements and some are questions, but all are designed to stimulate interest, elicit giggles, or generate a direct response. Using these icebreakers can help you make direct contact with any prospect you encounter, wherever you may be. Keep in mind that good opening lines, effectively delivered, may be all that it takes to start you on the road to happiness.

5. Following Up
and Closing the Deal

Okay, you've broken the ice. The prospect who has made your heart flutter at first sight has noticed you. Maybe your clever icebreaker has made that person laugh, smile, or respond positively. Or your attention-getting conversation starter has caused him or her to take the first step in breaking the ice with you. For whatever reason, you now have your prospect's undivided attention. Where do you go from here? To the follow-up, of course.

In order for you to quickly develop interesting, stimulating conversation, you must work initially within the context of the icebreaker. If this line directly focused on your prospect, stretch that icebreaker to include more conversation about your prospect. Minimize focus on yourself and keep the spotlight on the other person. Not only will this prevent you from seeming self-centered, the attention will flatter your prospect. However, if your prospect directs the conversation to you, then by all means feel free to talk about yourself. Just don't get carried away. After a reasonable amount of time, return the focus to your prospect.

In order to continue a conversation, you must be able to follow up your prospect's response. Naturally, this follow-up depends on the kind of response you get.

TYPES OF RESPONSES AND FOLLOW-UPS

People are unique, and their reactions to you can be equally unique. Your attempts at conversation can be met with responses that range from extremely positive to intensely negative. It's important for you to know when to respond and when not to, and when to continue your efforts or head for the hills. You should be able to masterfully handle virtually any type of response you get, whether it's a direct answer to a question, a sly innuendo, a snide comment, another question, a heated objection, or no response at all.

As you know, there are a number of different ways that prospects might respond to your icebreaker. Let's discuss some of the more common ones and include suggestions on how you might effectively follow them up.

Nonverbal Responses

What do you do if someone smiles, nods his or her head, or laughs at your opening question or line, but doesn't say anything? If you're nervous, your initial reaction may be to run. Don't. Give it another shot. Even a very simple question or statement can be useful:

☐ "What's your name?"

☐ "Do you like it here?"

☐ "It's pretty noisy in here; let me repeat my question."

Such follow-ups might be just enough to pave the way for additional exchange. Once your prospect has responded with something (anything!), move on to more open-ended types of questions and try to get a more meaningful conversation going.

If all your attempts are unsuccessful, then it's probably a good idea to move on. Don't view this as a rejection, and don't take it personally. In all likelihood, there are any number of reasons that the person may not have responded positively to you.

Brief Verbal Responses

If your prospect responds to you verbally, although briefly, at least you've got something to start with. Follow up specifically on the response. Either make a comment about the situation you're in, or ask a question designed to build upon the prospect's brief response:

☐ "Yes, this really is a nice place."

☐ "What do you mean by . . . ?"

☐ "Do you mean that . . . ?"

How do you know if the prospect's response is positive? Clues from their facial expression (a smile is more positive than a frown) and other body language (a back turned toward you is not a good sign) are good indicators. If the prospect continues to make eye contact with you, as if awaiting further conversation, it's probably safe to assume the response is positive.

Lengthy Verbal Responses

A more complete verbal response is certainly more encouraging than a brief one. After all, if the prospect isn't interested, he or she won't say anything to encourage further conversation. If you encounter such a positive response, you may want to go all out to solidify your contact. Ask interesting and relevant questions, make insightful comments, and show interest in what your prospect is saying:

- ☐ "I agree with you . . . "
- ☐ "That's an interesting point . . . "
- ☐ "What do you think about . . . ?"

The important thing is to keep the communication lines open and the conversation flowing.

Negative Verbal Responses

If your prospect responds negatively, you'll have to make the decision to either give it another shot or simply walk away. In all probability, your decision will be based on the type of negative response you receive. If you sense hostility, sarcasm, or a complete "closed door," you may choose to preserve your dignity, say something like, "Nice talking to you," and walk away.

If, on the other hand, the response is verbally negative, but the person still seems nice enough, you may want to give it one more try. Here, though, is where you should change directions. If you used humor in your opening line, try to be a little more sensitive and serious now:

- ☐ "Please forgive my comment/question. I just wanted to say hello, and I thought that my remark might have been the way to do it."

If you were serious initially (maybe too serious), try to lighten things up a little:

☐ "May I have a glass of water to wash down my foot?"

If this effort doesn't seem to open the door even a little, you may decide to simply cut your losses and move on.

Avoidance Responses

If your prospect totally avoids responding to you, there must be a reason. Maybe he or she doesn't speak your language! Maybe the person isn't interested in meeting anyone. Of course, there's always the possibility that the person is simply not interested in you. By now, though, you should be psychologically prepared to deal with that possibility.

Should you continue your attempt with this prospect? Probably not (unless you're in a noisy place and there's a possibility that your prospect didn't hear your line). You could, however, give it one last-ditch effort:

☐ "I'm really having a hard time. I like meeting and getting to know people, but it seems like people aren't responding. Would you please help me? Would you tell me what I'm doing wrong?"

And if this final attempt doesn't work, at least you'll know you tried. Don't get down on yourself. Give yourself credit for your determination and consider the experience a building block in the foundation of your self-esteem. There are plenty of other people out there for you to meet.

KEEPING THE CONVERSATION GOING

If you are like most people, you are probably worried about running out of things to say during a conversation. You may feel a pressure to keep the dialogue going because you think you'll be judged on your ability to keep talking. If the conversation stops, you might feel that it's your fault and your prospect will lose interest in you.

First of all, don't think that you're alone. Most people experience the same concern. It's important for you to realize that conversations are two-way streets. Your prospect has just as much responsibility as you do to keep the dialogue moving along.

However, instead of getting caught up in deciding who's responsible for the death of a conversation, let's discuss what you can do to keep it alive. Back in Chapter 4, we suggested that you jot down a few icebreakers and keep them in your wallet or pocketbook for handy reference. Well, you can use this same technique to keep a conversation flowing. On a separate card or paper, list a number of topics or subjects that you might introduce into a conversation.

Of course, we don't expect you to pull out the card in front of the other person and start reading. Be discreet. Excuse yourself and go into the bathroom where you can glance at the card. Try to memorize a few of the items (enough to solidify your blooming conversation). This will help you inject fresh topics into your exchange.

CLOSING TECHNIQUES

Let's say that you have gotten some communication going. At this point, you'll need to determine immediately how much time you have for conversation. You'll need enough time to "close the deal." In sales, this is called "closing the sale." It means wrapping up the deal—making the sale and creating a satisfied customer. Closing the deal in the context of this book means generating enough interest from your prospect to either make plans for a future meeting or, at the very least, exchange phone numbers.

Once the ice has been broken and a conversation is under

way, it's critical to get a feeling for how much time you have to close the deal. This time factor will help you decide on the particular closing technique you should use. Determining this time factor will help you gauge how long you have to speak with your prospect. It's up to you to get the right "feel" for the time factor involved. Your efforts to close the deal will fall short if you don't judge correctly. You don't want your dream prospect darting off and out of your life while you're still in the midst of making conversation!

Once you have determined how much time you have, you'll need to decide which of the three closing techniques you should use to wrap up the deal. They are the Quick-Close Technique, the Extended-Close Technique, and the Semi-Date Close Technique. Let's discuss these methods further and see how to apply each one.

Quick-Close Technique

The Quick-Close is described accurately by its name. If either you or your prospect are in a hurry (rushing to catch a train or trying to get to work, school, or a meeting on time), then the Quick-Close is the best technique. If you're in your car and pull up alongside an attractive prospect at a light, you won't have much time to close the deal, will you? This is another instance in which the Quick-Close should be used.

What's the best way to close the deal quickly? Be honest and direct. "I'd love to speak with you more, but it looks like you're in a hurry," or, "I'm in a rush to get to work/catch a train/get to class on time, but I'd really love to speak with you again." These lines must be followed by an attempt to make further contact: "Why don't you give me your phone number and let me know the best time to reach you." Then you should say something like, "I really enjoyed meeting you and look forward to speaking with you soon."

The following conversation, which takes place in a supermarket, illustrates the Quick-Close Technique:

Dave: How does a guy become a member of your fan club?

Kelli: I don't have a fan club.

Dave: You have one now. What's your name?

Kelli: Kelli.

Dave: I'm Dave. It's nice to meet you, Kelli.

Kelli: Thanks. It's nice to meet you, too.

Dave: I shop here regularly. How come I haven't seen you
before?

Kelli: I normally don't shop here. My sister and brother live
out this way. Tonight, we're having a twenty-fifth-
anniversary dinner party for my parents, and I needed
to pick up a few things. My sister is waiting for me so
we can start cooking.

Dave: What a nice thing to do. Listen, I don't want to keep
you. You're obviously in a hurry.

Kelli: Yes, I really am.

Dave: Kelli, I really enjoyed meeting you. And I'd love to
speak with you again, and also find out how the
dinner went. Can I call you?

Kelli: Sure. My number is 555-2421.

Dave: I hope your parents have a wonderful anniversary,
and I'll look forward to speaking with you soon.

Kelli: Likewise.

In this example, Dave used an icebreaker in his initial encounter with Kelli. He quickly determined that she was in a
hurry to get her parents' anniversary dinner started, so he

chose to use the Quick-Close. Besides Dave's highly complimentary opening icebreaker, he also praised Kelli and her siblings on their thoughtfulness in preparing a special dinner for their parents. Possibly the most important thing Dave did was let Kelli know that he wanted to talk to her again and find out how the dinner went. When using the Quick-Close Technique, it's critical to make sure that phone numbers are exchanged or a date has been made to insure future contact. (When Dave makes his follow-up call to Kelli, his conversation should touch upon her parents' reaction to the dinner, how many people were there, where it was held, if videos or pictures were taken, and so on.)

Also important in Dave's initial encounter with Kelli was his wish for the dinner to be successful. This further helped Dave to connect with Kelli, since he showed interest in something that was meaningful to her. Dinner together and the opportunity to see pictures or a video of that anniversary evening would be the perfect follow-up date.

Extended-Close Technique

The Extended-Close is ideally suited for situations in which you've determined that neither you nor your prospect are in a hurry. If you see that you can have ten or fifteen minutes (at least) of pleasant, pressure-free conversation, use the Extended-Close Technique. You'll have more than enough time to establish rapport, generate interest, develop a little chemistry, and either give or receive a phone number.

Let's go back to the grocery store and see how Dave uses the Extended-Close Technique in his first encounter with Kelli:

Dave: How does a guy become a member of your fan club?

Kelli: I don't have a fan club.

Dave: You have one now. What's your name?

Kelli: Kelli.

Dave: I'm Dave. It's nice to meet you, Kelli.

Kelli: Thanks. It's nice to meet you, too.

Dave: I shop here regularly. How come I haven't seen you before?

Kelli: Because I hate grocery shopping and do it only when absolutely necessary.

Dave: Is that the case today?

Kelli: Absolutely!

Dave: Well, Kelli, I'm glad you found it necessary to shop today. You've made it a very special shopping experience for me.

Kelli: (*Laughs*) Don't tell me that you actually like grocery shopping. Or do you?

Dave: I really don't mind it. I like to keep my refrigerator and cupboards stocked. I prefer to cook for myself rather than eat alone in a restaurant.

Kelli: What kind of foods do you like?

Dave: Mostly chicken, some fish, and just about all fresh vegetables. How about you?

Kelli: Pretty much the same, but I would have to add pizza and Thai food to the list.

Dave: I guess I forgot to mention pizza, but I've never had Thai food.

Kelli: Oh, Thai food is wonderful. It offers some very unique taste sensations.

Dave: Sounds interesting. I might like to try it. Is there a particular restaurant you go to for Thai food?

Kelli: As a matter of fact, there's a wonderful Thai restaurant that recently opened downtown.

Dave: Would you like to go there with me for dinner sometime?

Kelli: That invitation is hard to refuse.

Dave: Well, let me have your phone number and I'll call you later to firm up some dinner plans.

Kelli: All right. It's 555-2421.

Dave: When is the best time to call you?

Kelli: Most evenings between 8:00 and 10:00.

Dave: Great! Listen, Kelli, I really enjoyed meeting you and look forward to having dinner with you soon. I'll call you within the next couple of days.

Kelli: That's fine. I'll look forward to hearing from you.

This example shows how Dave, after breaking the ice with Kelli, was able to readily determine that this situation did not require the Quick-Close. At the end of Dave's compliment ("... you've made this a very special shopping experience for me."), Kelli laughed and then asked him a question. It was at this point that Dave figured he had enough time to employ the Extended-Close in his encounter with Kelli.

During the course of their conversation, Dave and Kelli "connected" on the topic of foods they liked. Furthermore, Dave zeroed in on Kelli's passion for Thai food and turned it into an offer for a dinner date, which Kelli accepted.

Semi-Date Close Technique

The closing technique that exemplifies the best case scenario is the Semi-Date Close Technique. This occurs when you meet an attractive prospect with whom you immediately seem to hit it off. Neither of you is under pressure to leave, and, because you are enjoying each other's company, you decide to go somewhere else together.

Let's say you meet someone while browsing in a bookstore, and then the two of you decide to go for a walk in the park. During your walk, you agree to stop for lunch at a local cafe. You have converted a casual meeting with your prospect into a semi-date. Of course, this may not be an "official" (prearranged) date, but such an impromptu experience has great odds of evolving into future official dates.

Let's see how our friend Dave uses the Semi-Date Close in his first encounter with Kelli:

Dave: How does a guy become a member of your fan club?

Kelli: I don't have a fan club.

Dave: You have one now. What's your name?

Kelli: Kelli.

Dave: I'm Dave. It's nice to meet you, Kelli.

Kelli: Thanks. It's nice to meet you, too.

Dave: I shop here regularly. How come I haven't seen you before?

Kelli: I don't know. I guess it's just been bad timing for you.

Dave: (*Laughs*) Yes, I suppose I should thank fate.

Kelli: Actually, you should probably thank my boss. I've got a certain amount of sick days from work, and I'm taking one today.

Dave: Are you sick?

Kelli: No, I'm just taking the day and glad that I'm not working.

Dave: I'm also glad you're not working.

Kelli: Well, thanks.

Dave: So what else have you got planned for the day?

Kelli: Well, I'm just picking up a few bare essentials here, then I figured I'd stop at the flea market around the corner and check out the bargains.

Dave: I love bargains. Would you mind if I joined you, Kelli?

Kelli: That would be nice. But don't you have to go to work today?

Dave: No. Today's my day off and I have nothing planned. As a matter of fact, I'd like to treat you to lunch after the flea market.

Kelli: Sounds okay to me.

Dave: Let's put the grocery bags in our cars, then we can walk to the flea market.

Kelli: Great idea, Dave. It's a beautiful day and I'd love the exercise.

Early in their coversation, Dave discovered that Kelli had the day off from work, so he quickly assessed that there was no pressure for the Quick-Close. When Kelli teased Dave about his "bad timing" at never having run into her before, Dave felt that Kelli was mildly flirting with him, so he was comfortable in continuing the conversation. It didn't take long for him to sense a mutual attraction, a rapport, so he decided to attempt the Semi-Date Close, which yielded positive results.

SUCCESSFULLY CLOSING THE DEAL

With today's fast-paced lifestyles, people are on the go much more than they might like to be. It is for this single reason that you should always be prepared to use the Quick-Close Technique in your encounters. It is likely that you'll meet many attractive prospects who won't be able to give you the time for much else. It's important for you to become a master of the Quick-Close. (Don't worry, there will also be those times when you'll have the luxury of additional time for nurturing a conversation and developing that all-important chemistry.)

When you have successfully mastered icebreaking, following up, and closing the deal with both the pressure on (the Quick-Close) and the pressure off (the Extended-Close or Semi-Date Close), you'll have gained the remarkable ability to meet many prospects anywhere and at any time. This accomplishment will play a dramatic role in changing the status of your single life forever. It will propel you into an active social life with potentially fulfilling relationships around each and every corner. This reason alone should be motivation for you to become a master at closing the deal.

IMPORTANT FOLLOW-UP CONVERSATION POINTS

During your conversations with prospects, keep the following points in mind. They will help stack the odds in your favor for a successful verbal exchange.

- Always get your prospect's name. And always give yours.

- During the course of conversation, be sure to casually use the other person's name.

- Always try to "connect" with your prospect on any subject or feeling. This common bond could cause a prospect to want to see you again.

- Try to identify your prospect's "hot buttons," then zero in on them.

No matter how difficult it may be for you to break the ice and carry on a conversation with a prospect, always remember that it gets better with practice. The more you get out there and talk to people, the easier and more natural it becomes.

WHERE TO GO FROM HERE

By now you should have a handle on some basic strategies that are helpful for starting a romantic encounter. You've packaged yourself desirably, you've worked on your attitude, and you are psyched to get out there and meet people. So, what's the next step? It is determining where "out there" is, and knowing what to do when you get there.

Now you are ready to move on to Part II of this book. It suggests specific avenues you can take to meet people, as well as particular places to go to find that certain someone. In addition, each section offers scores of icebreaking lines for you to use in specific situations.

6. Using Three Winning Techniques

*K*nowing where to go to find prospective love interests and being aware of effective ways to gain their attention is certainly valuable information when seeking a romantic encounter. In addition, you should be aware of three techniques that can be an asset to any successful program—the Seed-Planting Technique, the Laid-Back Technique, and the Use-of-Humor Technique.

SEED-PLANTING TECHNIQUE

Regardless of whether you see a prospect regularly or infrequently, you'll want that person to be aware that you find him or her desirable. Here's where you can implement the Seed-Planting Technique, which is a subtle way of letting people know you are attracted to them without making it seem like a come-on.

Simply plant little seeds of goodwill, friendliness, and mild attraction in the minds of your prospects. These "seeds" can range from a friendly hello that is accompanied by a nice smile and direct eye contact, to a pleasant line such as, "I'm lucky to have such a nice/pretty/handsome neighbor." Even a statement like, "You're my favorite cashier at this store," can plant a little seed of interest in that person. What you're really trying to communicate is that you like this person and find him or her attractive. And isn't that the message you want to convey?

It is important to remember the names of prospects you have met casually and are attracted to. When you see them a second time, be sure to address them by their first name. Most prospects will be flattered and impressed, especially if you don't see them often. People love when you remember their names. Also, as we discussed earlier, remembering the name of a prospect's friend, roommate, family member, pet dog or cat, etc., will score big-time points for you as a thoughtful, caring person. Chances are that these are precisely the qualities that are important to your prospect.

If you legitimately cannot remember your prospect's name, you can say something like, "I forgot your name, but I didn't forget what you look like. My name is ___. What's yours?" This straightforward, honest statement will certainly get the other person's attention.

If your prospect responds positively, the seeds you have planted will grow naturally. Other times the seeds may require some degree of nurturing. And of course, there will be those seeds that never mature due to any one of a number of reasons. Maybe the other person is already involved in a relationship or is simply not attracted to you. It is also possible that the person may have an attitude problem and may not be mentally capable of any romantic involvement. Such factors are beyond your control and should never discourage you from your seed-planting efforts.

Bear in mind that the subtlety of this technique does work effectively. For the best chance of successful results, keep a positive attitude that is both kind and sincere when planting the seeds.

LAID-BACK TECHNIQUE

Some people find it very effective to approach prospects in a laid-back, nonaggressive manner (at least during the beginning of their quest to meet prospects). If you find yourself at a dance club or bar and don't feel comfortable with immediately (and maybe obviously) looking for someone special, the Laid-Back Technique, which takes a nonassertive approach, may be a better, more natural way for you to meet others.

Here's an example of how you can employ this technique at a dance club. Shortly after you enter the club, get yourself a drink then find a comfortable seat in a highly visible area (close to the dance floor, at the bar, near the entrance to the rest rooms, etc.). Now sit back and let the prospects check *you* out. If they're interested, they'll approach you.

Keep your eyes open for prospects who are either cruising near you or who have relocated to a spot in your vicinity. Chances are that these people have noticed you and want to get a better look. As with most approaches, but in particular with this one, be sure to make eye contact and smile to encourage prospects to get closer to you. If you're interested in a prospect who seems to have noticed you and has moved nearby, try an icebreaker. As the prospect has already shown some interest, you'll be amazed at how easy and natural it will be for you to deliver the line.

Furthermore, with this approach you'll appear easy-going, relaxed, and self-confident—qualities that will make you more attractive. (By the way, don't be surprised if someone actually approaches you and attempts to break the ice first!)

USE-OF-HUMOR TECHNIQUE

Humor wins hearts! Let's face it, we all like to laugh. Laughter is free and one of life's greatest enjoyments. Why else are comedy clubs springing up all over the country? People usually enjoy your company if you can make them laugh. After all, it proves that you're a fun person to be with.

An incredibly simple and effective icebreaker, humor can be disarming as it helps a person relax and let down their guard. Of course, we're not prompting you to act like a clown or a cornball! What we are encouraging is that you become a fun person to be with by incorporating a little wit or humor into your personality. This will make the other person laugh or smile, and it lets them know that you enjoy talking to them.

There are times when you can initiate some humor through a curt, flirty line. Let's say that you're working out in a fitness club and spot an attractive prospect who is also working out. First, make eye contact and smile. Then, maybe say something like, "I don't know what's better for my health—my exercising or my watching you exercise!" Of course, make sure you deliver the line with a big smile on your face. Hopefully, you'll get a laugh. And if a conversation happens to develop, who knows where it might lead!

Harmless Self Put-Downs

Another way of using humor to your advantage is by poking fun at yourself. If done properly, this technique lets a prospect know that although you can be serious, you don't take yourself too seriously. Always make sure that the put-downs are delivered in a light, humorous way. After all, you don't want to make yourself look like a fool!

Let's say you want to use a humorous (yet harmless) self put-down as an icebreaker. Try walking up to your prospect with sad-looking puppy-dog eyes. With an exaggerated sigh say, "Hello. I have no life. Please have pity and talk to me." Delivered properly, this icebreaker could cause that person to chuckle, at the very least.

Maybe you and a prospect are having a conversation about the different seasons. You might inject some humor by saying, "I love the summer even though I usually don't have good luck in hot weather. I get buzzed by bees, constantly burn my feet on the sand, and always manage to drip ice cream on whatever I'm wearing."

If you're discussing sports with a prospect, you might say something like, "I'm interested in most sports, but I don't like going to baseball games. I've been to only two, but during those games I was hit in the head with a foul ball, needed oxygen due to the excessive heat and humidity at the stadium, and stained a perfectly good pair of jeans by sitting on some cotton candy that was stuck to my seat. It's safe to say that I can live without going to another baseball game. However, I'd be delighted to have you at my side at the football game on Sunday afternoon, provided I can bring along some protective gear!"

These examples show how you can humorously poke fun at yourself, yet still show a strong interest in getting together with your prospect. All it takes is a little creativity to incorporate this technique into your conversation.

Using Humor at Humorous Times

You can also use humor to your advantage by injecting a funny line at an appropriate time, even if it may seem to be during an inappropriate situation. For example, consider being in an elevator, a doctor's office, a dentist's office, or another place where soft background music is being played. If someone attractive is on the elevator or in such an office, you might say, "Excuse me, but would you care to dance? They're playing one of my favorites." You might accompany this line with arm and body motions that suggest dancing. The person will probably smile or break up laughing because your dance request is so absurdly inappropriate.

Here's an example of how humor helped break the ice for a gentleman who was attracted to the hostess of a restaurant he frequented. When she asked if he wanted the smoking or nonsmoking section, he first responded appropriately and then simply added, "And I'd like a table with an ocean view." (Of course, there was no such view anywhere in the restaurant.) She laughed and directed him to a table. During his meal, the hostess stopped to see how he was enjoying the "view." At this point, he got her involved in a bit more conversation, and by the time he left the restaurant, he had her phone number.

Still another way of winning hearts through humor is by telling a joke. A joke is always good for loosening up people and getting the happy feelings flowing. Furthermore, it is an indication that you're fun to be with.

Remember, when using humor to break the ice, your goal is to get the prospect to smile or laugh. If you make your first impression memorable by causing an immediate amused reaction, you could simultaneously be creating a foundation for future laughing and loving with your new prospect.

7. Breaking the Ice
With Attention Getters

*L*ike many people, you may cringe at the thought of having to use a line to meet an attractive prospect. Why? It could be due to a fear of rejection or finding yourself at a loss for words. It could also stem from a concern that you'll come off sounding desperate, aggressive, corny, hokey, or insincere.

Here's the good news! There are ways to initiate an encounter with a person without having to say a word. For example, wearing a flashy hat or a funny T-shirt can compel a prospect to speak to you. It's a great way to shift the burden of starting a conversation into the hands of interesting prospects.

The following icebreaking attention getters are designed to attract prospects and get them to start a conversation with you. You won't have to say a word to generate the initial contact. Prospects will be encouraged to approach you, wherever you may be. Although there are many creative things you can do to achieve this attention, we have focused on some of the more interesting examples.

BOOKS AND MAGAZINES

Carry a book or magazine with a fascinating title. The more interesting the title, the more likely it is to produce a comment or query from a prospect. Be sure to carry or read the book in a way that leaves the front cover exposed, and be sure to take it everywhere you go.

Women may choose to carry books and magazines that might appeal to men. Examples of such magazines include *Sports Illustrated, Baseball Digest, Car and Driver*, and *Popular Mechanics*. Good book choices might include *Jordan Rules, Sting Like a Bee, Wealth Without Risk,* and *How I Made a Million Dollars in Mail Order*.

Men might choose to read or carry magazines that would pique a woman's interest enough to cause her to make a comment. Magazines such as *Gourmet, Travel & Leisure*, and *New Yorker* are good choices. Book selections might include *Zen Macrobiotic Cooking, Success Forces, Life's Little Instruction Book,* and *Aliens Among Us*. These and plenty of other books or magazines are likely to evoke comments and spark conversations.

By the way, if you happen to see a possible prospect reading an interesting book or magazine, don't let the opportunity pass you by to break the ice with a comment of your own. Express your interest in the book or magazine and, rest assured, a conversation will follow. Carry on from there!

SIGNS

The written word can certainly attract attention. So why not put some well-constructed thoughts on a cardboard sign? Watch the attention you get with this tactic!

What should your sign say? Well, you might write the first

part of a joke or riddle and invite the reader to supply the punchline. Or you might ask a trivia question, again trying to elicit the answer from curious passersby. You might decide to print a blowup of a personal ad for all in your vicinity to see. If you are artistic, you can draw or paint something really elaborate and eye-catching. The artistic composition alone could cause people to comment.

Prop the sign next to you on a counter or chair, attach it to a stick, hang it around your neck, or wear it on your back. Just beware: If your sign is interesting and easy to read, you're going to attract attention like a magnet!

BUTTONS

Sport a button that makes a statement, asks a question, or touts your personal cause, then sit back and be prepared for some responses. Your button might say Single and Miserable, Party Animal, My Lawyer Can Beat Up Your Lawyer, Lose Weight Now. . . Ask Me How, Ask Me What Planet I'm On, Help the Homeless, Save the Animals, and so on. Make sure the buttons are large enough to read and interesting enough to provoke a response.

TEE SHIRTS

Wear tee shirts in outlandish colors with something interesting written on them. Things like the name of your favorite band, vacation spots, and television shows are good choices to display on tee shirts. Otherwise, an interesting slogan, saying, or even a picture will attract attention.

PETS

Take your dog for leisurely walks through your neighborhood

(or any neighborhood for that matter). You never know who you'll run into. If you take the dog to a park or beach, bring a toy for it to play with. Be sure to throw the ball or toy near any attractive prospects you see in order to attract their attention.

Although any type of dog can be a good conversation starter, unique breeds are even better. Another good idea is to fasten a big bow or brightly colored bandanna around the dog's neck, and you're in business. If you don't have a dog, borrow one from a relative, neighbor, or friend.

This technique for starting a conversation can also work with other pets, like cats and birds, although you'll have to be careful of what you do and where you go. It's certainly not a good idea to take your bird for a walk in the park!

KIDS

Kids provide great material for conversations. On the weekend, take your child/children/nephew/niece/neighbor's child once removed, out to the park, playground, or beach for an afternoon of fun. Don't be surprised at how often you are approached by divorced or other single parents. Keep in mind that men and women with kids always seem easy to approach.

HATS

Looking for attention? Wear a snazzy, fashionable, or outrageous hat and you're apt to get lots of comments. If you have a face for hats and a flair for the creative, give this idea a fling.

HEADBANDS

If you jog, work out, dance, or are involved in any sports activity, wear a brightly colored headband to draw attention. If the band bears the name of your favorite sports team, that's even better. You may get comments from prospects who either love or hate your team. Either response is fine as long as it promotes some interaction.

CAMCORDERS OR CAMERAS

Go to a park or beach with your camcorder or camera. They're great conversation starters. When a prospect breaks the ice and asks what you're filming or taking pictures of, be ready with an interesting response that will initiate a conversation. If you're somewhat aggressive, you could respond to the question with something like, "I'm creating an album on the beauty of nature, and I think you're a natural beauty. I'd love to include a picture of you in my album."

If you have your pet with you, approach a prospect and ask if he or she would please take a picture of you with your pet. In appreciation of the favor, offer to treat the person to an ice cream cone or even lunch! Even better, offer to take a picture of your prospect and promise to mail a copy to him or her. When you send the photo, be sure to include a short, warm note.

TRAVEL BROCHURES

Carry travel brochures with you to work, meeting places, restaurants, or other public places. They are great conversation starters. Lay them out or carry them in plain view. While you leaf through the brochures, don't be surprised if people who happen to be nearby begin to comment. They may ask you questions, offer suggestions ("I hear there's a fabulous seafood restaurant there called . . . "), or share a personal experience or two that they had while vacationing in the same location.

TIES AND SOCKS

Looking to draw some attention to yourself and get a conversation started at the same time? Put on a pair of outrageously designed, wildly colored socks, or a vibrant, flashy tie. Not only are items such as these fun additions to your wardrobe, they are sure-fire attention getters as well.

SPORTS EQUIPMENT

Plan a sports outing with some of your friends. Tennis, volleyball, baseball, basketball, and biking are good choices. Before and/or after the outing, plan to stop somewhere for a meal or snack. Be sure to carry your equipment into the snack bar or restaurant and place it on the table or counter. The sight of the equipment will more than likely elicit responses from other customers.

HAIRSTYLES

Try a new hairstyle! In order to generate attention, try something different or even outrageous. Men, try growing a ponytail or pigtail. If your hair is normally short, grow it long. If you are used to wearing long hair, get a crew cut or shave your head. Grow or remove beards and mustaches. Try anything to change your appearance.

Women, dye or rinse your hair an outrageous color. Grow it long, cut it short, braid it, curl it, or adorn it with pretty barrettes. Try anything to draw interest and comments from men.

KITES

Perfect to fly at a beach or park, kites are great attention getters and conversation starters. Don't get upset if you can't seem to keep your kite airborne; an attractive prospect may offer to help. And don't forget, you can always use this opportunity to seek help from a passerby (the right passerby, of course).

BUTTON COVERS

Attractive, attention-getting button covers are a great new way to dress up shirts and blouses. The button covers, which come in unique shapes and unusual designs, clip onto existing buttons to add spark and pizzazz to outfits. Try these unique oufit enhancers to generate interest from others.

These are just a few of the many ways to effectively get yourself noticed. Try out the ones that you feel most comfortable with. And remember, these attention-getting strategies are limited only by your sense of adventure and imagination.

Part II
Making Contact

8. Choosing Contact Sites and Functions

S ingle people have a myriad of places and events where they can meet other people. Regardless of whether these places and events are designed specifically for singles or are instead intended for anyone who enjoys socializing, there are many opportunities available. In any of the categories that we'll be discussing in Part II, consider a "singles oriented" designation to be a bonus. And remember, as you become more confident in using your techniques, you'll increase your chances of meeting someone in virtually any setting.

The various singles events and co-ed endeavors that you'll be reading about are designed solely to bring singles together and are categorized as "singles oriented sites and functions." Many people laughingly refer to them as "singles dysfunctions." This may be because some people believe that a high number of dysfunctional individuals come to these events. But other, more enterprising singles find that these functions offer a wealth of opportunities for meeting prospects. Try some. What do you have to lose? Remember, you need to connect with just one person. Don't be discouraged, even if there are rooms full of nothing but unappealing people.

If you're not currently participating in any singles activities, you're passing up good opportunities to meet prospects. Singles get-togethers are designed to provide fun and the chance to meet other unattached people. By getting out to these kinds of functions and activities, you may develop a new interest or hobby, make a new friend, or, best of all, find the love of your life.

In addition to events sponsored by or specifically for singles, there are groups, clubs, meetings, and classes designed for people in general that you can attend or join in the hopes of meeting single prospects. Also, your daily life may regularly put you in situations where you interact with single people.

HOW TO FIND INFORMATION

Let's say you feel that some of the sites and functions suggested in Part II are great for you. However, you're wondering how to find out what clubs, organizations, or resources in your area you should check with to put the suggestions into action. The best place to start is the Singles Calendar of Events column in your local newspaper. Many newspapers feature a special section on certain days that's a sort of What's Happening/Upcoming Events/Things to Do/Weekend Activities roundup. Often, listings of singles activities are included. Almost every contact site and function you'll be reading about in this book will be mentioned at some time. Also, read magazines in your areas of interest, since they, too, may have columns or advertisements describing singles functions or special events.

Check with local health, civic, and community organizations, which have information on what regular activities are available locally and what special events are coming up. Local libraries also have a wealth of information that will help you decide what you want to do and when.

And, of course, you can speak to other singles, to find out what they're doing. Not only would you get details about what opportunities exist and how you can get involved, but just asking for information is a great opening gambit to meet prospects.

THERE'S NO LIMIT TO THE POSSIBILITIES

You're probably anticipating some of the sites and functions we'll be discussing, but others may surprise you. For each situation, we'll include suggestions for icebreaking lines that might be useful in these specific settings. Of course, the lines given are only the tip of the iceberg. They're really offered just to stimulate you to start thinking of your own lines. As with the lines suggested in Part I, you can modify them for use in other situations. Make sure that when you use a line, however, you feel comfortable saying it. Otherwise, it won't help you. In any situation, remember the two steps to meeting and developing a relationship with someone—break the ice, then follow up.

The message is clear—you can meet someone and start a romantic encounter just about anywhere! Yes, it requires effort, but it's worthwhile if you find someone. So, let's discuss possible places and events where you can start moving in the right direction.

9. Singles Dances
and Parties

Among the most popular functions for meeting singles at are dances and parties. Dances and parties can be found at just about any time of the year. They can be especially helpful for meeting prospects during the holiday season (see Chapter 23).

SINGLES DANCES

Singles dances have always been popular for bringing together large numbers of eager people. The best dances are the ones that are sponsored either by a religious organization or by a group that runs dances professionally.

You will be more apt to find someone of your own faith at a dance sponsored by a religious organization. If you're concerned about potential problems down the road involving religious beliefs and child rearing, this may be a good path to follow.

There are also singles dances designed to draw a wider selection of prospects. Organizations sponsoring these dances place less emphasis on religious beliefs and more on bringing in healthy admission fees and packing the hall with singles.

Many people meet and connect at singles dances, so these affairs should never be overlooked. However, if you're shy, you may feel uncomfortable approaching desirable prospects unless you have practiced and prepared beforehand. So, spend the necessary time practicing your lines and preparing for a variety of reactions to your approach, and just plan on having fun (and enjoying the music!).

Lines for Singles Dances

☐ "I'd really love to dance this one with you."

☐ "Could you save a slow dance for me?"

☐ "The turnout is fantastic tonight, isn't it?"

☐ "Every time I see you, you're wearing the same thing." (*This humorous line is for use with someone you've never seen before.*)

☐ "I didn't realize they were having a beauty pageant tonight. Where are the rest of the contestants?"

DANCE CLUBS

Dance clubs, of course, will always draw throngs of singles for the purposes of dancing, drinking, and meeting someone new. It's not surprising, though, that many singles do not care for dance clubs due to the heavy crowds, the smoke-filled rooms, and the superficial nature of many of the people who go. This doesn't mean that you can't meet someone at one of these clubs. And you could always use this setting as a place to practice your lines!

Lines for Dance Clubs

☐ "Would you share a dance with me? Back in high school, my friends called me Crazy Legs Muldansky/the Disco Kid."

☐ "Do you think the music is loud enough?"
(*This line works well when the music is deafeningly loud and you say it directly into your prospect's ear. It usually produces a laugh and breaks the ice.*)

☐ "Would you like to get out of this smoke and get a cup of coffee?"

☐ "What's your sign? My sign's go!"

SQUARE DANCES

Square dances can be lots of fun and are often loaded with singles. If you want to meet an attractive single prospect, this is a great place to do-se-do.

Learning to square dance is relatively easy, so most people, even those with two left feet, can pick up the basic steps within minutes. Since you'll be swinging from partner to partner when you square dance, be sure to focus on the dancers you want to meet. You can also mozy on over and strike up a conversation on the sidelines while your prospect is resting.

Lines for Square Dances

☐ "I love the way you square dance."

☐ "You have some great square-dancing moves."

☐ "You must be square dancing for years. You do it so effortlessly."

☐ "I don't know you, but can I choose you to be my square-dancing partner?"

☐ "I feel so square, having not square danced with you yet."

☐ "I'd love to square dance this one with you."

☐ "Would you join me for a good square meal after this square dance?"

☐ "You're the one person I've been wanting to dance/speak with all night."

SINGLES PARTIES

Singles parties are a great way to meet attractive prospects. Some singles parties are run by local companies whose specific business is to sponsor these events, while others (such as the Meeting Group Party out of St. Louis, Missouri) are run by companies that travel throughout the nation sponsoring parties. The admission fee for most singles parties is fifteen dollars or more, depending on whether food is served and what the actual nature of the event is. The parties are usually held at large hotels such as the Holiday Inn, Sheraton, or Hilton, which are easily accessible and have plenty of parking.

Some singles parties have themes, and some are distinctive for the way the participants are encouraged to meet each other. For example, at one type of party, once your admission fee is paid, you are given a name tag and a corresponding partner to seek out and start a conversation with. You may be Scarlett according to your name tag and should find Rhett somewhere among the partygoers. Or Punch may search for Judy, Fred may look for Ginger, Fric may seek out Frac, and so on. When you find your designated name-tag partner (as well as any other prospects), you'll have the option of enjoying light conversation, dancing, eating, drinking, playing board games such as backgammon or checkers, or following the lead of the emcee in any fun game or activity. Another twist at some singles parties is that you may be required to bring a guest of the opposite sex to the party. This insures a larger turnout of singles and also a more equal ratio of men to women.

The Meeting Group Party, mentioned above, has a more sophisticated approach. For your admission fee, you receive a name tag and a handful of small cards. On the front of the cards you write your first name and phone number, while on the back of the card you check off printed messages such as: "I enjoyed speaking with you; I'd like to speak with you some more." "I didn't get a chance to talk to you but I'd like to, so here's my number; call me."

There are a couple of basic conditions all Meeting Group partygoers must adhere to. You are not permitted to refuse a card from anyone. This is designed to eliminate any direct rejection. Also, you should circulate. The emcee of the party, who keeps the party going and flowing, continually urges partygoers to keep meeting prospects for brief conversations of about five to fifteen minutes. During these short conversations, cards can be exchanged. This is a great way to meet everyone you find interesting—since this is already being encouraged by the emcee and the meeting group.

Lines for Singles Parties

☐ "When I saw you, I felt compelled to mingle with you. I took advanced mingling in college."

☐ "I'd really love to talk to you."

☐ "If I can't mingle with you, I want my admission fee back."

☐ "I would give you my birth certificate if I didn't have any cards left."

SINGLES HOUSE PARTIES

Singles house parties are another way to meet interesting people. These kinds of parties, usually for a specific age range, are often advertised in local newspapers for particular dates and times. All you pay is a small cover charge at the door to reimburse the host for the food and drinks.

Singles house parties are informal get-togethers of motivated singles who generally do not like the club scene. They prefer, instead, to meet other unattached people in a casual, homey atmosphere. If you haven't tried a house party yet, you should definitely attend one. In addition, if you have the room—and the nerve—throw your own house party.

Lines for Singles House Parties

☐ "This livingroom is wonderful! I feel like I'm home."

☐ "Would you like to take a look at the patio/backyard/balcony?"

☐ "This couch makes me feel like I'm sitting on a cloud."

☐ "Trade you!"
   (*This line should be said while offering the prospect some Hershey's Kisses.*)

SINGLES POOL PARTIES

A swimming pool environment is another great place for singles to meet. Singles can get together to enjoy swimming at a daytime function that includes lunch and mingling. Or, pool partygoers can gather in the evening, dressed casually and chatting poolside, with cocktails and munchies. With a back-drop of candlelit tables and a moonlight ambiance, nighttime pool parties make a very romantic setting to meet a special prospect.

Singles who enjoy swimming may also find prospects at their local public pool, college campus pool, or area swim club.

Lines for Singles Pool Parties

☐ "The moon, the pool, and you—what a romantic trio."

☐ "I love the way the moonlight is bouncing off your hair."

☐ "Can I get you a towel?"

☐ "Was your father a thief?" (*Wait for response.*) "Because he stole the stars right out of the sky and put them in your eyes."

SINGLES LUNCHEONS AND DINNERS

Singles luncheons and dinners are where hordes of singles spend from ten to twenty-five (or more) dollars to join other singles for a one-time lunch or dinner. The quality of the food varies, depending upon the restaurant or caterer, but the food is not the purpose of the event. Go to a singles luncheon or dinner because you are hungry for a mate, not a meal. If the food is good, consider it a bonus.

Singles luncheons and dinners are often buffet-style, so that singles can eat what they want, when they want, and wherever they want. Here is a sure-fire five-step method for successfully mingling, meeting, and dining at buffet-style affairs (this method can be used as well at other singles activities):

1. Scan the room to find the prospects who appeal to you the most. Mentally target, in order of priority, the two or three

prospects you most want to meet. If you see more than three prospects, keep the remainder as back-ups in case your first three prospects do not work out.

2. Sit down at the table of prospect number one, with only a first course such as a bowl of soup or a salad. Remember, if you intend to meet single prospects in this fashion, you must sit at their table, or at one nearby, to be able to strike up a conversation.

3. If prospect number one responds to you in a positive manner, after you go back to the buffet to get your next course, return to the same table to further the rapport. Or, ask the prospect if he or she would like to join you at the buffet or if there is anything you could bring back. This will aid in developing a bond with your prospect.

4. If your attempts with prospect number one prove unsuccessful, no matter what the reason, return to the buffet for your next course but, with your plate of food in hand, go to the table of prospect number two. You can say, "Somebody took my seat at the other table. Is it okay if I pull up an empty chair here?" Or, "You look interesting. I thought I'd join you for lunch/dinner." Or, "Do you mind if I break bread with you?" Proceed as you did before—try to start a conversation, create a rapport, and develop some chemistry.

5. If you are unsuccessful with prospect number two, get more food or some dessert and coffee from the buffet, then go to prospect number three's table and proceed as before.

Incidentally, even if something positive develops with one prospect, you can still try to meet other prospects. Just ask for the first prospect's phone number and say that you look forward to speaking again soon. Excuse yourself, go back to the buffet for more food or dessert, then sit down at the table of a new prospect.

The purpose of buffet-style luncheons and dinners is two-fold. Essentially, the buffet format allows you to meet as many prospects as possible, while also giving you a way out when you find yourself sitting with someone who you realize you are not interested in or who has no interest in you. By the way, try not to take too much food each time you go to the buffet table or you'll find yourself stuffed very quickly!

In the unlikely event that the singles luncheon or dinner is not set up buffet-style, scan the room for your number-one choice of a prospect immediately upon entering so that you can get a seat in a good location. Then try your best to establish a rapport and make a connection either during or after the meal.

Lines for Singles Luncheons and Dinners

☐ "Isn't this great food?"

☐ "Which salad dressing would you recommend?"

☐ "What is that on your plate? It looks delicious!"

☐ "This clam chowder/roast beef/chocolate cake is wonderful! I highly recommend it."

WEDDINGS AND ENGAGEMENT PARTIES

Weddings and engagement parties generally bring out all the single friends, neighbors, and family members of the bride and groom. Many of these singles, usually the friends of the new or soon-to-be husband and wife, may be just as eager as you are to meet someone and join the ranks of their married friends. This is why scouting for attractive single prospects at weddings and engagement parties can be so productive.

The single people at wedding-related functions are happy, in a festive mood, looking their best, and interested in meeting someone for a relationship that may one day lead to marriage. Besides the singles attending the wedding or engagement party as guests, prospects may also be found working at the affair. Some of the jobs that singles may be found doing include photographer, wedding coordinator, caterer, food server, floral arranger, musician, and coat checker. If you attend a wedding in the right frame of mind, you'll often meet someone new.

Lines for Weddings and Engagement Parties

☐ "You'd make a beautiful bride/handsome groom."

☐ "I think I'll be ready to settle down after this wedding."

☐ "I love the beautiful floral arrangements/table settings."

☐ "Is my tie straight/cummerbund crooked/slip showing?"

☐ "I don't think I've ever been to such a festive wedding."

☐ "I hope I can find someone to make me as happy as the newlyweds are with each other."

☐ "I'd love to ask the photographer to take a picture of you/us together."

☐ "Every time I go to a wedding, I feel so happy for the newlyweds. Then I come home and feel empty because I don't have anyone to share those happy feelings with."

10. Entertainment Sites

*T*here are many entertainment sites where singles can meet. The following are only a few of the possibilities. Read through them and then see if you can come up with others.

SINGLES GAME NIGHTS

Singles game nights are a fun way to get out and meet prospects. Game nights involve a selection of activities including cards (such as pinochle, gin rummy, poker, and bridge), board games (such as backgammon, checkers, chess, Scrabble, and Monopoly), and other games (such as Yahtzee, ping pong, pool, and air hockey). Bingo nights, often held in churches or under other organizational sponsorship, also fit in this category.

The idea at singles game nights is to find an interesting prospect and to engage in any one of a number of games with that person, either individually or as part of a group. Game nights are wonderful for helping singles to connect with each other and also to establish a shared interest in specific games or activities. If you like playing cards or games and are looking for someone to share your life, singles game nights are a must for you.

Lines for Singles Game Nights

☐ "Would you like to share this game with me?"

☐ "Would you be interested in being my partner for this game?"

☐ "We need another player for this game. Would you be interested?"

☐ "I bet that spending time with you would be even more fun than this game."

MUSIC FESTIVALS AND CONCERTS

A great place to meet singles is at a music festival or concert. Music festivals and concerts frequently offer an open-air atmosphere, with live musical groups, dancing, related merchandise, and refreshments. Besides working there, singles can be found attending the show or participating in any number of activities, so keep your eyes open for appealing prospects.

Country music, which is currently enjoying a popularity craze, has become a big draw for singles. For this reason, country music clubs are springing up all over the place. If you're looking to find prospects who also enjoy country music, or you just want to get out, kick up your heels, and have a grand old time, visit a country music club and enjoy yourself.

Whether you like country, rock and roll, rap, jazz, classical, folk, or any other type of music, you'll find music-related outings teeming with singles being moved by the sounds of their favorite recording artists. Since music generally has a positive effect on the spirit, mind, and physical being, chances are that the prospects you approach will be happy and receptive to you, especially since you're sharing their musical interest. Also, listening to your favorite music can help you, too, feel good all over and will add to the positive energy you'll exude when you approach prospects in these surroundings. Finding someone special who appreciates the wonderful feelings that come from music can truly add to your life.

Lines for Music Festivals and Concerts

☐ "Do you have any of their cassettes or CD's?"

☐ "What's your favorite song/album by them?"

☐ "Have you been to any other music festivals/concerts?"

☐ "I'm not sure if I'm smiling because I love the music or because I'm enjoying looking at you."

☐ "Would you join me in sharing some positive musical vibes?"

☐ "The best part of this festival/concert has been meeting you."

☐ "Can I buy you a Coke/Perrier/hot dog/slice of quiche/tee shirt?"

☐ "This music is giving me an out-of-body experience."

MOVIE THEATERS

Movie theaters are a really good place to find single prospects. Single people often get together with friends or go by themselves to see a movie. They do this just to get out because they do not have a date or because they are lonely and bored sitting at home. Look for prospects standing in the ticket line, waiting at the concession stand, milling in the lobby before or after the movie, sitting in the theater before the movie starts, or exiting the building.

Movies are popular for dates. For this reason, it is best to approach only those prospects you are sure are out with friends or by themselves! If you work it right, you might see a terrific film and also meet an equally terrific prospect.

Lines for Movie Theaters

☐ "What movie are you going to see?"
(*This line should be used only in multiplex theaters; otherwise, you'll sound pretty foolish!*)

☐ "Have you heard any reviews about this movie?"

☐ "All of a sudden, I wish I was seeing whatever movie you're going to be seeing."

☐ "I hate waiting in ticket lines. I'm a terrible waiter."

☐ "What did you think of the movie?"

☐ "I'll buy the popcorn if you buy the drinks."

☐ "I'll let you cut in front of me in line if you join me for the movie/treat me to some popcorn."

JAZZ CLUBS

Jazz music has always been known as the music of choice of ultra hip, super cool people. Now that mainstream society has come to accept jazz, singles everywhere are taking to jazz clubs on a regular basis. Jazz is soothing and relaxing, yet very distinctive. Many single jazz aficionados are attractive while also unique. Appreciating jazz is definitely a worthwhile credential for a single prospect.

Lines for Jazz Clubs

☐ "Have you always been into jazz?"

☐ "Jazz is the best. It's so relaxing."

☐ "I've heard about an upcoming jazz festival. Have you ever been to one?"

☐ "Who are your favorite jazz recording artists?"

☐ "What do you think of this group?"

KARAOKE SING-ALONGS

Karaoke sing-alongs, which originated in Japan, are one of the newest ways to get out and meet other singles. Before a sing-along gets under way, you are given a list of the song options. There are hundreds of songs to choose from. You check off your selections, then return the form to the disc jockey or Karaoke master of ceremonies. During the sing-along, when a song is selected for play, the words to the song appear on a giant screen and the background music (just the music, no vocals) begins to play. If you are one of the people who selected the song, then you are a singer! Sing the words that appear on the screen.

Some establishments have the singing participants gather on the dance floor or stage; some let the participants sing from their seats. Try to scan the audience as soon as you arrive to see if there are any attractive prospects. And remember—location, location, location! You must be within striking distance of your prospect to make successful contact. No matter where your prospect is singing from (the dance floor, the stage, or his or her seat), you must be in close proximity. While you are singing, you can try to make eye contact and smile at your prospect. When the song is over, a conversation hopefully will ensue. If not, you can use an opening line to break the ice.

Karaoke sing-alongs are currently being featured at many nightclubs and restaurant bars throughout the country. For these businesses, they are generating a major flow of customer traffic, which increases the profits. For single people, they are another way to increase the odds of meeting a promising prospect.

Lines for Karaoke Sing-Alongs

☐ "Have you ever sung at one of these before?"

☐ "You have a wonderful singing voice. Are you a professional singer?"

☐ "Your voice is beautiful. Would you sing me a lullaby?"

☐ "What's your favorite song? I'd sing it, but then it probably wouldn't be your favorite any more!"

11. Organizational Work

*T*here are many organizations you can do volunteer work for, both to help the organization and to forward your efforts to meet singles. If you have a favorite charity or civic group, find out how you can get involved with it. If you're not sure what group you'd like to join, speak to other people. Check under "Organizations," "Charities," or "Associations" (among other headings) in the Yellow Pages, or ask your local librarian for suggestions. Let's discuss some examples in this category.

CHARITABLE GROUPS

A fine way to meet singles is to join a charitable group. A success story in this category involves an independent twenty-four-year-old single woman named Shawn. Here's her story:

One committee that I'm on is for the American Heart Association. Every year, my county's chapter has a bachelor auction fund raiser. This is the second year in a row that I'll be in the Bachelor Recruiting Department. What a great way to meet single men! I've dated a couple of the guys here and there. Nothing serious, but a good time. Recently, for this year's auction, some people at work told me to recruit their friend. He is thirty years old, good looking, and owns a dry cleaner here in town. I called him, introduced myself, and told him why I was calling. I stopped by his store one night to give him details about the bachelor auction. He was receptive to the whole idea. I told him I'd get back to him for the interview we'd have to do.

Needless to say, I have disqualified him from the auction. For the past month, we've been an item, and at this point, neither one of us is interested in having him in the auction! Maybe I have never met anyone in a supermarket or library, but silly me, I was definitely taking my clothes to the wrong dry cleaners. I've been working less than a mile away from him for two years. A lot of "finding the right people" is being involved in committees like I am. I strongly urge this for single women. Plus, you are doing things for the community and society. You use your time wisely (not in bars), and you feel good because you do something worthwhile.

There are other ways you can get involved with charitable groups. You can join volunteer committees that work to raise funds, increase public awareness, or enlist support for organizations such as the Arthritis Foundation, Leukemia Society, AIDS Foundation, Lupus Foundation, and American Cancer Society. Other charitable groups aid the homeless, help underprivileged children, or fight world hunger. Volunteering your time will not only help your chosen organization in its efforts but can put you in touch with other singles who have similar concerns and values. Furthermore, as a "do gooder," you will generate positive energy, which will help you to attract quality prospects.

Singles are out there, and there's a good chance that you'll meet the right prospect if you get involved with a charitable group. And even if there are no other singles on your volunteer committee, you may be able to network yourself into meeting an eligible prospect through a new-found committee friend.

Lines for Charitable Groups

☐ "I can't believe you're interested in this cause. It's so important to me."

☐ "I am going to file an official protest if I don't find an open seat next to you at our next meeting."

☐ "Did you see today's newspaper?"
(*This line is for use when an article of interest to your charitable group was included in the newspaper.*)

ENVIRONMENTAL GROUPS

Many people are sincerely concerned, and even outraged, over what the human race has done to the environment. They join environmental groups, which try to help protect the world from the damages of air pollution, acid rain, nuclear radiation, ocean dumping, littering, and so on. Singles who join causes such as these care enough about the world to lobby the government as a group for a safer environment, or to stand up and be heard individually at local meetings and public rallies. Chances are that the prospects you would meet fighting for the environment would be persons with the right kind of values.

Lines for Environmental Groups

☐ "What got you interested in this organization?"

☐ "Weren't you at the rally downtown/at City Hall/in Washington last year?"

☐ "The environment is a great reason to meet you. Though any reason would be a great reason to meet *you*."

ANIMAL RIGHTS GROUPS

Many singles get involved with animal rights groups, along with the related meetings, rallies, protests, and marches. If you are a single animal lover, you will meet other concerned singles who believe in the humane treatment of all animals. Associations in this category include People for the Ethical Treatment of Animals (PETA), Friends of Animals, the Humane Society, and the Doris Day Animal Welfare League. All of these groups provide situations where animal-loving singles can meet, mingle, and bond.

Lines for Animal Rights Groups

☐ "How long have you been working with this organization?"

☐ "I am really glad I came tonight. I love animals so much, and I feel I can actually do some good with this group."

☐ "Do you have any pets at home?"

COMMUNITY GROUPS

Many singles are community-oriented and enjoy being involved in their neighborhood or town. Therefore, an excellent way to meet geographically desirable singles is to join a community group. You can either get involved in the planning end of community events or just be a participant. Examples of some local events are bazaars, parades, fairs, festivals, auctions, block parties, and celebrations for holidays such as the Fourth of July, Thanksgiving, New Year's Day, and Labor Day.

Keep abreast of local events. Note dates and locations on your calendar. If you can, try to get involved in helping to plan them; at the least, attend them. You undoubtedly will meet some singles.

Lines for Community Groups

☐ "I can't think of anyone I'd rather have in my group."

☐ "This committee needs rounding out—you could supply the beauty/brains/humor."

☐ "I love this town, and I'm really enjoying doing something valuable for it."

☐ "I recently moved here. Do you know a good place to meet singles?"

☐ "It's great to meet someone nice from this area. I also was born, bred, and buttered here."

POLITICAL GROUPS AND COMMITTEES

Another fine way to meet singles is to join a political group or committee. Political affiliations, such as the Republican and Democratic parties, have meetings, rallies, voter registration drives, cocktail parties, and the like, where many politically oriented singles can be found. You can also join a political committee, where you can work with other singles for the election of a specific candidate or support of a certain cause.

If you are single and like politics, be sure to get involved in a political group or committee. You'll increase your odds of meeting prospects with parallel political interests. Also, make it a priority to vote during all major and local elections. After you've voted, stick around the polling station to meet attractive prospects. You can discuss the election and politics with anyone you find interesting.

Lines for Political Groups and Committees

☐ "I'm glad that you're on our team."

☐ "I want to be a member of whatever political party you're affiliated with."

☐ "I'd like to nominate you for President/State Senator/County Commissioner."

☐ "Have you seen a blue sport coat/red sweater/brown purse lying around somewhere?"

12. Dining

*D*ining is considered to be one of our greatest pleasures. As such, places for dining are naturals as settings to meet and then develop relationships with interesting prospects. Let's discuss different types of dining establishments and how to take advantage of them.

RESTAURANTS

Dining out in restaurants is popular among single people. It's a fantastic way to meet other singles while at the same time enjoying a meal. The following are types of restaurants where you would be more likely to find single prospects.

Pizza Parlors

If you like pizza (and even if you don't!), an ideal spot to find single prospects is your local pizza parlor. Since pizza is satisfying, quick, and easy, many singles go to local pizza parlors on a regular basis. Those who get their pizza delivered miss opportunities to meet attractive prospects who eat at the parlor to enjoy their pizza fresh from the oven. Even if you just pick up your pizza instead of having it delivered, you will have a chance to meet prospects also picking up pizza, just arriving to eat in, just leaving, or working at the restaurant.

Lines for Pizza Parlors

☐ "Come join me at my table for some pizza."

☐ "Can I pull up at your table? I'll bring the drinks."

☐ "I'm taking a poll. What's your favorite pizza topping?"

☐ "I would sacrifice my last slice of pepperoni to meet you."

Diners and Coffee Shops

Other eateries popular with singles are diners and coffee shops. These establishments fit in perfectly with the single lifestyle because they generally aren't fancy or expensive. They often have counters where you can sit down and eat your meal next to other singles. This is very conducive to starting an informal conversation. Also, because the diner/coffee shop atmosphere is down-home and friendly, starting a conversation with someone seated in a booth while you're standing, with someone standing while you're seated, or even between booth and counter is not that difficult.

You can find single prospects waiting in line to be seated, following the host or hostess to a seat, seated at the counter or in a booth, walking to the rest room, using the pay phone, and waiting to pay their checks at the cashier's stand. Single prospects are everywhere in this type of restaurant, and it's up to you to meet them.

Lines for Diners and Coffee Shops

☐ "Do you have any suggestions on what to order? You look very trustworthy."

☐ "That looks wonderful. What are you having?"

☐ "You're sitting in my favorite seat at the counter/in my favorite booth. Did you slip the maitre d' some cash to get it?"

☐ "I love diner food. It's just like mom used to make—only without the nagging!"

☐ "The instant I saw you, my heart and the cheese on my sandwich both started to melt."

☐ "I don't know what you're ordering, but if you help me select something from the menu, maybe we could share."

Fast Food Restaurants

Because of their fast-paced lifestyle, many singles grab a quick meal at their favorite fast food restaurant. To meet and connect with other singles at such establishments, you'll need to avoid the drive-through window and go into the restaurant. You can find single prospects standing in line, standing at the fixin's bar, seated, and even working behind the counter.

Fast food restaurants are everywhere. The best time to meet other singles is at mealtime, but anytime is a good time.

Lines for Fast Food Restaurants

☐ "Can I do the fixin's for you?"

☐ "Let me help you get all that stuff back to your table."

☐ "I'd like to recommend the roast duckling."

☐ "You look like a small fries/large fries/nonfries kind of person."

☐ "I've seen salad bars with less stuff than this fixin's bar."

☐ "I'm afraid I'm going to have to issue you a citation for excess lettuce/onions/tomatoes/ketchup being dropped on the fixin's table."

Fun Eateries

Fun eateries are popping up all over the country. The atmosphere is lighthearted, with music and interesting artifacts adorning the restaurant walls. The food is good, and it's served without much of a wait. There is also usually a bar, where you'll find plenty of singles loosening up with a drink before sitting down to their meal. Examples of this type of restaurant are the popular national chains TGI Fridays, Houlihans, Bennigans, Ground Round, and Fuddruckers. In addition, many local, privately owned fun eateries have probably already cropped up in your home town.

Check the restaurant guide in your local newspaper for a listing of these restaurants. Also, find out if the local shopping malls have any. Singles are attracted to fun eateries, so find out about all the places in your area. You'll be glad you made the effort.

Lines for Fun Eateries

☐ "Where did you hear about this place?"

☐ "Have you eaten here before? I come strictly for the frogs' legs. I've found that a cup of coffee plus an order of frogs' legs really gets me hopping through the rest of the day."

☐ "The sight of you warmed my heart and my cup of coffee."

☐ "Please join me at my table. I'll buff and shine the seat. I'll dust away any crumbs. Whatever it takes to make you feel comfortable."

☐ "I've been so anxious to meet you that I've actually been hoping you would start choking on food so that I could perform the Heimlich maneuver, save you, and introduce myself."

Specialty Restaurants

Specialty restaurants, such as Italian, Chinese, seafood, and gourmet eateries, are ideal places for singles to find prospects. Go into one of these restaurants with the right kind of attitude—a positive one—and chances are that you'll have a delightful meal plus meet someone special.

Lines for Specialty Restaurants

☐ "What's your favorite type of restaurant?"

☐ "Have you eaten here before?"

☐ "What's the specialty of the house?"

☐ "What's a nice girl/guy like you doing in a nice place like this without a nice guy/girl like me?"

SALAD BARS

Salad bars are excellent spots to look for single prospects. You'll find singles busily filling their salad plates with a variety of different vegetables, fruits, and toppings. Many spend time contemplating what to add next; "salad loading" can be a major decision for some singles. Since most people, however, visit the salad bar just briefly to fix up their salad and then go right back to their seat to eat it, your mission here, should you decide to accept it, is to approach a prospect first and fill up your salad plate last. Take your salad plate and head directly over to an attractive prospect. You'll need to act quickly before your prospect is "salad loaded" and ready to return to his or her seat. Start fixing your salad near your prospect and make your move.

Lines for Salad Bars

- [ ] "Do you know what the different salad dressings are?"

- [ ] "That looks like a wonderful salad."

- [ ] "You scoop very neatly. I'm extremely impressed. Where did you learn how to scoop like that?"

- [ ] "How do you fill your salad plate without banging your head on this apparatus? I already have a mild concussion."
(*This line is for use at salad bars with overhead lighting units.*)

- [ ] "Every time I go to the salad bar, one of the restaurant staff has to clean up after me."

- [ ] "How did I get so lucky to find you in my salad bar line?"

- [ ] "I'll scoop veggies for you if you dip dressing for me. I took Scooping 101 in college."

- [ ] "Will you scoop for me while I hold my plate/hold my plate while I scoop? I can't walk and chew gum at the same time."

SINGLES BARBECUES AND PICNICS

Barbecues and picnics are always fun. Singles barbecues and picnics are a fine way to get out and meet other singles during warm weather. They are frequently advertised and usually have a more than adequate turnout of single prospects. Combine a relaxing afternoon, the warm sun, and comfort food with the possibility of meeting a wonderful new person, and you've got a winning situation.

Lines for Singles Barbecues and Picnics

☐ "Can I get you a hot dog/hamburger/drink/napkin?"

☐ "I would be delighted to hold your ear of corn while you nibble."

☐ "I, along with the ants that are sharing my picnic table/blanket, would be very happy to have you join us."

☐ "Excuse me, but would you please allow me to protect you from any grasshoppers or bees with bad attitudes?"

SINGLES DINING CLUBS

Singles dining clubs are a terrific way to meet single prospects and, at the same time, dine out at some of the finer restaurants in your area. Single people have the opportunity to join other unattached people in enjoying elegant, exceptional, exciting, and exotic meals.

Membership in a singles dining club brings with it a wide array of monthly events. Some dining clubs also offer travel packages to cities around the United States or abroad for unique culinary experiences. If you like to eat, dining clubs are a great way to meet prospects.

Information on singles dining clubs can be obtained from singles newspapers and magazines, and from food and gourmet magazines, all of which are available at newsstands and bookstores. Also, look in the food or restaurant section of your local newspaper, or in the listing of area singles activities.

Lines for Singles Dining Clubs

☐ "How long have you been a member of this club?"

☐ "How does this restaurant compare to others where you've eaten?"

☐ "Have you belonged to any other clubs?"

☐ "I don't know about you, but I feel fate has put our culinary appetites together."

☐ "Is there a club you can join where singles share indigestion problems from dining out?"

13. Business and Professional Activities

*T*he workplace has always been a handy site for singles to meet because of the convenience factor. In a work environment, it is very natural for a relationship to develop and flourish. Many companies create opportunities for singles to meet and mingle with one another by organizing softball games where different departments within the company play against each other. Some companies also belong to leagues, which pit local companies of many specialties against one another and open up all sorts of horizons as far as prospects are concerned. Company parties at holiday time offer further opportunities for singles within the same firm to connect.

A major drawback of work-initiated personal relationships is that they sometimes affect the work relationship. An employer-employee relationship may bring about jealousy or charges of favoritism from coworkers. Also, if the personal relationship goes sour, so may the work relationship; uneasy feelings may be prevalent in one or both parties, which can make things awkward for everyone in the office. Jobs can sometimes even be jeopardized. You should clearly evaluate the ramifications of a workplace romance before you allow yourself to become immersed in such a relationship.

Now let's discuss some of the specific settings in which work can contribute to fun.

INDUSTRY MIXERS, WORKSHOPS, AND SEMINARS

An excellent way to meet singles in your field of work is attending an industry mixer, workshop, or seminar. Regardless of your field, chances are that industry mixers are held periodically to bring together people from all facets of the industry; many of these people are single. Often, wine and cheese parties are held to afford people a casual atmosphere for meeting, mingling, and developing new professional and personal relationships.

Industry workshops and seminars may also be offered to help you further develop your expertise and increase your knowledge in specific aspects of your industry. Workshops and seminars are often attended by sharp singles who are looking for career advancement and an increase in their net income.

If you are single and in a specific field, be sure to check your trade journals for the dates of industry mixers, workshops, and seminars. You will increase your skills, enlarge your network of professional acquaintances, and possibly meet an attractive prospect in your field.

Lines for Industry Mixers, Workshops, and Seminars

☐ "What facet of this industry are you in?"

☐ "Are you planning on attending any industry workshops/seminars? Maybe we could go to one together."

☐ "Is this your first industry workshop/seminar?"

☐ "Are there any cassettes available for this workshop/seminar?"

☐ "I'm planning on buying the corresponding cassettes for this workshop/seminar. If you're not getting them, I'd be glad to make copies for you."

☐ "Will they be serving coffee and Danish during break? It's not an official break without coffee and Danish."

CONVENTIONS AND TRADE SHOWS

In some fields of work, attending or exhibiting at conventions or trade shows may be a part of your job. At conventions and trade shows, single people can be found selling their company's product or service, buying products or services for their company, or just furthering their product knowledge. Opportunities abound for singles with common interests to meet and connect.

Additionally, if you have an interest in any careers other than your own, you could attend a convention or trade show and possibly meet singles from totally unrelated fields. There are trade shows for just about every kind of business imaginable. You can find books and magazines at your local library that list the various trade shows and conventions for the entire year.

Lines for Conventions and Trade Shows

☐ "How long have you been in this line of work?"

☐ "I've been in this field for a few years now. How come I've never had the pleasure of meeting you before?"

☐ "How often do you attend these shows?"

PART-TIME JOBS

If you are single and could use some extra money (and who couldn't?), try working a part-time job in a high traffic area with repeat customers, such as a gas station, restaurant, or convenience store. This type of work situation will put you in contact with a multitude of people, many of whom will be single. Also a good choice would be a part-time job connected with one of your hobbies or areas of interest; for example, if you're a bicycling enthusiast, you could meet like-minded prospects through a part-time job at your local bicycle store.

Lines for Part-Time Jobs

☐ "What made you decide to take this job?"

☐ "Have you ever thought of working full-time?"

14. Outdoor Activities

Meeting new people can be like inhaling a breath of fresh air. And what better place to get that breath of fresh air than in the great outdoors? If you like to commune with nature and want to share your experiences with new friends, consider the many different outdoor activities that are available.

BEACHES AND POOLS

Beaches and pools have always been known as great places for meeting other singles. Beaches are mainly a summertime meeting place, unless you're in a southern clime, so you have to make the most of them during the proper season. Of course, not all parts of the country have beaches, but more and more resort areas are building their own—even without oceans!

You'll probably have better access to pools on a year-round

basis, since both indoor and outdoor pools will serve your purpose. Town pools, and even pools at local hotels, can be a great site for singles, if you don't have friends with backyard pools.

Slip into your most happening swimwear and make something happen. Pick a prime location and set up camp. Bring out all your gear—beach blanket, Frisbee, sunblock, suntan lotion, cooler, radio, book, magazines—whatever it takes to get yourself comfortable. Then pick out some prospects and make your move. If the response you get is not to your liking, go for a walk. You'll find hordes of singles sunbathing, reading books or magazines, playing Frisbee or paddleball, walking, swimming, eating, or drinking, and each and every one will be a potential prospect.

Lines for Beaches and Pools

☐ "Can I get you a towel/drink/some munchies?"

☐ "Can I pull up a lounge chair/blanket next to you?"

☐ "Will you join me for a walk on the beach?"

☐ "May I double-park on your sand for a while?"

☐ "Meeting you here at the beach makes me want to have sand between my toes for a very long time."

☐ "Have there been any attacks on swimmers/surfers by sharks or crazed tuna?"

☐ "You have the best looking swimsuit at the pool/on the beach."

☐ "My feet are burning up from the sun and sand. Would you like to go in the water for a little while?"

☐ "Do you know why some suntan lotions/sunblocks are proud that they have PABA while others advertise that they're PABA-free?"

☐ "How often should you reapply suntan lotion/sunblock on an average day at the beach?"

☐ "Could you please tell me the secret of applying suntan lotion/sunblock without gluing sand to your entire body?"

☐ "Could you spare some ice for my water bottle?"
(*This line is for use with a prospect who has a cooler.*)

☐ "Your shoulders are getting burned. Could I help you apply some lotion?"

PARKS

Whether they're in the country or the city, parks have a pleasant, restful, stress-free atmosphere. Take a walk in your local park and you're apt to encounter singles relaxing on benches, walking dogs, reading books or magazines, lounging on the grass, sunbathing, or taking a lunch break. Around lunchtime, parks usually draw a good crowd of single people.

Scan the park for prospects and pick out the best location for making contact with the most appealing. Or, park yourself on a bench that prospects who are walking or bicycling will have to pass. Perhaps you will be "discovered" by an attractive prospect because you were in the right location to be seen. You can also walk your dog, if you have one, since dogs are phenomenal conversation starters.

It's always a good idea to bring along a book. If you're "reading," any contact you make will seem accidental or natural, as opposed to contrived. You'll look as though you came to the park to read and relax, when in actuality, you cleverly were there to go prospecting!

Lines for Parks

☐ "Is this a beautiful day or what?"

☐ "What are you reading? It looks interesting."

☐ "Will you join me for a walk in the park?"

☐ "You certainly know how to shake the leaves off my tree." (*This line works best in the autumn.*)

☐ "I hope the rest of my day looks as good as you do." (*This line is for use in the morning or at lunchtime.*)

☐ "It's so nice to see a beautiful woman/handsome man like you on such a beautiful day."

SINGLES CAMPING TRIPS

Singles camping trips are a great way to meet prospects who are outdoorsy and nature-loving. But you've got to like sleeping in tents and be pretty much oblivious to bugs.

Many singles love camping and "roughing it." If you do, make yourself available for the next singles camping excursion and nuzzle up to your favorite prospect over a toasty campfire.

Lines for Singles Camping Trips

☐ "Would you allow me to be your guide through camp?"

☐ "Would you join me in the mess hall for ____?" (*Insert appropriate meal.*)

☐ "You're just the type of person I like to roast marshmallows with."

SINGLES HAY RIDES

Singles hay rides are a classic way to meet fun-loving prospects. People have been going on hay rides and meeting this way for years. The informal nature of a hay ride lends itself to a casual atmosphere where conversation is easy.

A new type of hay ride is the "haunted hay ride," in which riders are driven through a farm, field, or forest area where scary creatures are supposedly prowling. Of course, you'll want to get close to, and snuggle up with, someone you like. Hence, haunted hay rides can be effective at bringing singles together.

Lines for Singles Hay Rides

☐ "Have you ever been on a hay ride before?"

☐ "I can't think of anyone I'd rather be on a hay ride with than you."

☐ "Either this hay is itchy or I have a bad case of fleas."

☐ "Would you protect me from monsters?"
   (*This line is for use on haunted hay rides.*)

BICYCLING CLUBS, BICYCLING TOURS, AND BIKE-A-THONS

Bicycling is an incredible way to meet interesting singles. Besides being fun, it's ideal for promoting optimum health and an increased life span.

Singles interested in bicycling and in meeting other single cyclists can join bicycling clubs or participate in cycling tours or bike-a-thons. Bicycling clubs offer cyclists an opportunity to socialize at club meetings and on bicycling excursions to scenic and fascinating places. Bicycling tours are generally open to the public and are sponsored by bicycling clubs as a way to enlist new club members. Bike-a-thons are often sponsored by charities to help raise money.

While many singles bicycle for personal health and enjoyment, many others also pedal to prospect, which is exactly what you should do if you're single and love bicycling. Look for attractive prospects at bicycle club meetings, at the starting and finishing lines of sponsored events, while bicycling, and at rest stops and check points.

Lines for Bicycling Clubs, Bicycling Tours, and Bike-A-Thons

☐ "Would you mind if I ride along with you?"

☐ "This is a really nice area. Have you ever biked here before?"

☐ "Can I buy you some juice at the next rest stop?"

☐ "I love your bandage. Is it Ralph Lauren or Armani?"
   (*This line is for use with a bicyclist sporting a bandage.*)

☐ "I can't think of anyone I'd rather have blocking my wind."

☐ "Are your buns hurting as much as mine from this bicycle ride?"

WALKING CLUBS, WALKFESTS, AND WALK-A-THONS

Walking is another wonderful form of exercise. It's excellent for singles who want a good cardiovascular workout with a limited risk for injury. Any time you go for a walk, you have a chance to meet other people. Just keep your eyes open and be ready and willing to strike up a conversation with passersby.

The opportunity to meet other singles who enjoy walking or PowerWalking (a brisk form of walking) can be found by joining a walking club or attending a walkfest or walk-a-thon. Walkfests and walk-a-thons are usually sponsored by charities such as the American Diabetes Association, Multiple Sclerosis Society, and American Heart Association. They are usually held to raise money for research, in addition to offering people, many of whom are single, a fun day of walking for fitness.

You can also volunteer to work at a walkfest or walk-a-thon.

You could help at the registration table or at a rest stop, where attractive single walkers may ask you for assistance.

Serious walkers can take this activity one step further by joining walking clubs. Club meetings provide dates and times of local planned walks, organize walking excursions, provide information on types of walking shoes, and the like. So, if you're interested in walking, here's a way to enjoy a hobby as well as possibly meet a love interest. Just stroll on over and make your move.

Lines for Walking Clubs, Walkfests, and Walk-A-Thons

☐ "Do you mind if I walk along with you?"

☐ "Nice walking shoes. What brand are they?"

☐ "Watch out for that pothole/cracked pavement/dog poop!"

☐ "Where did you learn to walk like that? You have some great moves."

☐ "Your feet must be really tired. You've been running/walking through my mind all day."

SKYDIVING AND MOUNTAIN CLIMBING CLUBS

For those singles who are more adventurous than most, there are activities such as skydiving and mountain climbing, and there are clubs you can join to meet singles with these similar interests. If you are single and like to walk the fine line, these—and many other activities—might be of interest to you.

15. Trips

Who says that the only place to meet singles is where you live? There are many wonderful opportunities to meet singles if you like to travel. Sometimes, the reduced pressure when you are away from the hustle and bustle of your normal activities can increase your chances of making new relationships flourish.

SINGLES WEEKEND GET-AWAYS

Singles weekend get-aways are an option available to single people who want to get away from their surroundings for a combination minivacation and opportunity to meet other singles. There is generally a wide range of carefully planned activities available designed to help introduce participants. All you have to do is get involved in any activity that interests you, and you will meet prospects.

Singles weekend get-aways are a lot of fun, but they are still just a vacation. Enjoy them as such, and try not to have any further expectations. If you are lucky, you will meet someone who lives within train or cruise-control distance of your home town.

Lines for Singles Weekend Get-Aways

☐ "Where did you hear about this trip?"

☐ "Have you ever gone on a get-away before?"

SINGLES VACATIONS

Another opportunity to be considered is the singles vacation. Singles vacations generally range anywhere from four nights and five days to two full weeks. They are booked by travel agencies and usually offer a variety of exciting vacation spots around the world as the destination. Examples of vacation programs that cater to the whims and needs of single people are Club Med and Hedonism, although there are many other programs available, too.

Singles vacation programs offer unattached people the opportunity to spend their vacation time having fun with other singles. The only possible drawback is that these vacations are booked by singles from all over the country and maybe the world. Therefore, you may very well meet and share some quality time with a prospect, but the prospect may turn out to live far away from you. If this does not pose a problem for you, however, go for it! Singles vacations can be a great way to spend your vacation time.

Lines for Singles Vacations

☐ "Have you ever come to one of these resorts before?"

☐ "All of a sudden, this vacation is looking a lot better."

SINGLES TOURS

Singles tours are similar to singles vacations but have sight-seeing or touring of interesting landmarks as their primary goal. This, then, is an ideal way to travel to exciting far-away places or historical landmarks and at the same time share the experience with other singles who also enjoy traveling. A love of traveling will be the common denominator between you and the single prospects you meet. If you are single and love to travel, this is one avenue you should definitely explore.

Lines for Singles Tours

☐ "Did you enjoy history when you were in school? I figure that's why you're on this tour."

☐ "Have you traveled with any other tour groups?"

SINGLES CRUISES

Singles cruises are another option for unattached people, one that many think is the most relaxing way to travel. Some singles cruises are just one-day outings. An example is an evening river cruise, where a large group of local singles meets to mingle under romantic moonlight. This type of singles cruise generally features food and dancing, along with a host of opportunities to meet prospects in a dressy evening atmosphere. It is very similar to a singles party or a singles luncheon or dinner, and you can use the steps and lines described on pages 82–84 to make contact with prospects.

Another type of singles cruise is the vacation cruise, which is usually booked through a travel agent. The travel agent will work through a tour packager such as Single World, which organizes groups of singles and books them onto Norwegian, Carnival, or Royal Caribbean cruise ships. You can cruise to any number of lovely island paradises for up to two weeks. If desired, you can share a cabin (and the expense) with a roommate who has been matched to you according to gender, age, and smoking habits. The food on a cruise is usually excellent, and the complete jam-packed schedule of activities is hard to believe. Singles who have taken cruises have found them to be wonderful vacations even if they don't produce a love connection. For more information, contact your local travel agent or Single World (1–800–223–6490).

Lines for Singles Cruises

☐ "One look at you and I don't think that I could ever be seasick."

☐ "How did you find out about this cruise?"

☐ "I wouldn't mind gazing at you through my porthole."

☐ "Would you join me for ____?"
(*Insert appropriate meal.*)

☐ "I don't know what I'd rather do—gaze at the stars above or gaze at you."
(*This line is for use on clear evenings.*)

ADULT SINGLES CAMPS

Adult singles camps are where single adults can go to enjoy a weekend, week, or more of sleep-away-camp fun and games. Many, if not most, of the camp activities are designed to bring singles together.

Adult singles camps are similar to singles cruises and singles weekend get-aways except for the atmosphere. Campers generally sleep in cots, eat in a mess hall, and wear jeans. You can meet other singles while hiking through the woods, roasting marshmallows over the campfire, participating in a craft workshop, playing a team sport, or participating in a myriad of other social events. Activities generally run from early in the morning until late in the evening and provide a wide range of choices to cater to most everyone's tastes.

The adult singles camp atmosphere is low-key and unpretentious, so you will likely meet down-to-earth prospects. If you liked camp as a child, chances are you'll love camp for single adults.

Lines for Adult Singles Camps

☐ "Is my marshmallow supposed to catch on fire like this, or just get brown?"

☐ "I feel like Hansel and Gretel. Stay with me, and I'll protect you from the witch!"
(*This line is for use during a hike in the woods.*)

☐ "I like the outfit you're wearing. It looks comfortable, functional—and sets off your eyes."

SINGLES GAMBLING JUNKETS

Singles gambling junkets are for singles who love to gamble. Sign up for a bus, train, or plane ride to Las Vegas, Reno, or Atlantic City for a day or weekend of gambling at one of the many prominent gaming establishments. Also on the junket will be other singles who love the action and the environment. You'll be able to meet prospects traveling to and back, while gambling, during dinner, or while participating in any other activity with your group.

Lines for Singles Gambling Junkets

☐ "One look at you, and I feel like I'm going to have good luck at the tables."

☐ "I'd love to have you right at my side for good luck."

☐ "Would you like to try your luck and join me for ____?" (*Insert appropriate meal.*)

RETREATS

Many people, including singles, go on retreats. Retreats offer quiet, contemplative, and relaxing therapeutic atmospheres away from the topsy-turvy real world. You may unexpectedly find the perfect companion while unwinding at a retreat. If you don't, you'll be well-rested and refreshed for meeting prospects when you return home.

Retreats are frequently sponsored by religious organizations, so you can inquire about them at your house of worship.

Lines for Retreats

☐ "Isn't this quiet wonderful?"

☐ "Would you like to join me for a stroll in the garden/around the lake/in the woods?"

16. Sports

M any singles are into fitness, health, and athletics. Sports activities, therefore, are natural forums for similar-minded singles to meet one another.

SPORTS OUTINGS AND LEAGUES

There is an ever-increasing need for creative ways to bring singles together. Since many single people have at least a marginal interest in sports, while others are sports fanatics, it stands to reason that sports outings and leagues are an ideal way to bring singles together. The following sports are currently the most popular.

Softball

Softball games are primarily held in warm weather and bring

out a good crowd. Men generally like softball, and women looking to meet single men will find plenty of them here.

Lines for Softball

☐ "We play great together. You and I should start our own league."

☐ "You look great out there in the field. You're a natural."

☐ "It wouldn't be a softball game without you here."

☐ "You can use my glove/bat. I only lend it to special people."

☐ "I can't help but admire your speed and grace as a base runner."

Volleyball and Walleyball

Volleyball and walleyball games are wonderful for meeting prospects. The main difference between the two games is that you play walleyball in an enclosed racquetball court and can bounce the ball off any of the walls within the court. Since both games require a team effort, a lot of new friendships and relationships can develop. In both games, your position on the playing court rotates due to the frequent change of servers. This creates many opportunities for you to meet prospects on both your team and the opposing team. Also, in subsequent games with different teams, as well as in between or after games, many opportunities exist to make new connections. You can also join volleyball and walleyball leagues, which will help bring you in touch with other singles who enjoy these sports.

Lines for Volleyball and Walleyball

☐ "I may not know you, but I want you on my team."

☐ "Can I buy you a drink after our game?"

☐ "How long have you been playing volleyball/walleyball?"

☐ "You give our volleyball/walleyball team a good look."

☐ "You have a great kill shot."

☐ "I definitely want you on all my volleyball/walleyball teams."

Bowling

If you like to bowl, another way to meet prospects is to attend singles bowling outings or to join a singles bowling league. Singles bowling outings are one-time events designed to bring singles together. Even if you've never bowled or aren't particularly thrilled with the sport, it's still worthwhile to attend one of these outings. Many singles show up, more because they are interested in finding someone special than they are in impressing others with their bowling skills. If you're a decent bowler, it's a plus, but it's not necessary for a singles bowling outing.

The same is true for singles bowling leagues. The only difference is that singles bowling leagues are for singles who truly enjoy bowling, since leagues play regularly, on a specific day every week. It doesn't matter what your skill level is, just as long as you enjoy bowling.

Lines for Bowling

☐ "How long have you been bowling?"

☐ "What's your bowling average?"

☐ "I would gladly polish your bowling ball or buff your shoes."

☐ "You may not knock down a lot of pins, but you've sure bowled me over."

Tennis

Singles tennis outings are specifically for singles who enjoy the game of tennis. Tennis is a sport that is enjoyed with equal interest by women and men, so there are often large turnouts for tennis outings. Get your tennis racquet out of the closet, throw on some sporty tennis wear, and sign up for some singles tennis. You may be surprised to learn that you can love tennis and fall in love with a tennis-loving prospect both at the same time.

Lines for Tennis

☐ "How long have you been playing tennis?"

☐ "What type of racquet do you prefer—regular or oversized?"

☐ "You have a great tennis style. If I take you out to dinner, would you give me some lessons?"

☐ "Would you be interested in being my doubles partner?"

☐ "What type of court surface do you prefer?"

☐ "What type of sneakers do you find best for playing tennis?"

☐ "Have you ever played on a _____ court?"
(*Insert type of surface.*)

Skiing

Skiing has always been a popular sport among single people. Therefore, singles ski weekends tend to draw a wonderful crowd of single ski buffs. Skiing is an excellent sport and requires quite a bit of athleticism. For this reason, you will probably meet athletic, well-conditioned prospects. You can find prospects on the ski lift, on the slopes, in front of the lodge fireplace sipping hot chocolate, and even in the infirmary! You can also join a ski club, where you can regularly meet singles who share your interest in the sport.

Lines for Skiing

☐ "How long have you been skiing?"

☐ "Can I get you a cup of hot ____?"
(*Insert beverage.*)

☐ "Consider me your personal ski slope attendant if you wipe out anywhere near me."

☐ "Would you believe that I planned this injury just to meet you?"
(*This line is for use in the infirmary.*)

☐ "Do you know any good local places to eat/go dancing?"

☐ "I'm looking forward to seeing you on the slopes. Actually, I'm looking forward to seeing you anywhere."

Golf

Golf is one of Americans' favorite games. It's also a favorite game of singles for two good reasons—it's easy to be placed in a foursome with other singles, and once you are thrown together with new people, you have plenty of time to get to know them. Check with your local golf courses to find out how they pair their golfers and if they have special "tee-off" times for singles. Then grab your clubs and start swinging!

If you are a duffer with relatively little experience, there's nothing wrong with signing up for golf lessons, either at the golf course or in an adult education setting (see page 135). You may find that there are other singles with the same idea, and you may start meeting prospects even before you get out on the links!

Lines for Golf

☐ "How long have you been playing golf?"

☐ "What's your handicap?"

☐ "Where did you learn to play golf like that?"

☐ "There's nothing like the game of golf to get you to enjoy the outdoors."

☐ "I used to get really teed off. Now all I do is tee off!"

SPORTING EVENTS

If you are a sports fan, then going out to a live sporting event to root for your local team is an excellent way to meet prospects. Cheering for the home team or just showing an interest in a particular sport can be enough to get a relationship going.

Lines for Sporting Events

☐ "How long have you rooted for this team?"

☐ "Do you come to many games?"

☐ "Would you be interested in joining our tailgating party?"

SPORTS BARS

Single people who enjoy nightlife should check out the fast-growing crop of sports bars in their local area. Sports bars are usually colorful watering holes that feature walls adorned with sports memorabilia, giant-screen televisions, lots of video and electronic sports games, and sports-themed dance floors. There are various ways to start up conversations and countless things to do with prospects. Sports bars are terrific sites for meeting other singles and having fun at the same time.

Lines for Sports Bars

☐ "Would you like to share a snack while we watch our team devour the opponents?"

☐ "Our team can't lose with you rooting for them."

☐ "Would you join me for a halftime dance?"

17. Hobbies and
Self-Help

O ur society is very much involved with self-improvement and pleasure. Most people enjoy spending time
on hobbies and other activities of interest. But why
spend time on these activities alone? Why not try to combine
the pleasure you get from these activities with the chance to
meet some interesting prospects?

ARTS AND CRAFTS FAIRS, FESTIVALS, AND SHOWS

Many people have an intense interest in arts and crafts, and
there are many places where you can enjoy this hobby as well
as meet singles. For example, you could visit an arts and crafts
fair, festival, or show, all of which feature a variety of artists
and craftsmen displaying their wares or goods such as fine arts,
pottery, jewelry, leather, woodwork, baskets, fabrics, furniture,
and blown glass. Events such as these are a great way to spend

a day. Singles can be found selling wares, shopping, and browsing.

Similar to arts and crafts fairs, festivals, and shows are antique fairs, which are extremely popular in certain parts of the United States. Single antique buffs can enjoy meeting and mingling at these events.

Lines for Arts and Crafts Fairs, Festivals, and Shows

☐ "Would you like to join me as I window shop?"

☐ "What do you think of this as a birthday gift for my ____?" (*Insert name of friend or relative.*)

☐ "I desperately need to get a last-minute gift for an artsy friend. You look like you've got good taste. Would you have any suggestions for me?"

MUSEUMS AND ART GALLERIES

Museums and art galleries can be fascinating places to meet prospects. Take some positive action and get out to one of these cultural centers. Make yourself presentable, put on your glasses, and act reasonably cultured.

When you go to a museum or gallery, don't be intimidated by the surroundings. The atmosphere is quiet and reserved, but this is because most of the visitors are concentrating on the exhibits. Communication is by no means prohibited; you can, and should, talk to other people, especially singles. For example, while sauntering through the museum or gallery, let's say you notice a very attractive person admiring a piece of art. As you admire this attractive person, you can sidle up next to him or her and make a clever statement. Speak about how fine art stands up to the test of time and that you've been depressed ever since your pet turtle destroyed your Andy Warhol rendition of Arnold Stang. It was the only piece of fine art in your collection that you really cherished.

All types of art museums, as well as museums of sports memorabilia, rock and roll, classic cars, wildlife, and other themes, are ideal places to meet interesting singles. You can find singles admiring the exhibits, paying admission, checking the directory, entering or leaving the rest rooms, or standing in the lobby.

Lines for Museums and Art Galleries

☐ "Have you ever seen anything more beautiful?"

☐ "I see you're admiring this unusual painting. What do you think of it?"

☐ "Have you seen any other work by this artist?"

☐ "I find it amazing that anyone could produce something like this. I'm all thumbs myself."

COLLEGE AND ADULT EDUCATION COURSES AND WORKSHOPS

There's nothing like a good education to enhance one's life. And there's nothing like an educational setting for meeting singles. Besides pursuing an advanced degree, many single people attend college or adult education courses or workshops to meet other singles with similar interests. Take a course in painting, sculpting, jewelry making, or cooking, and you'll be amazed at how many singles you'll find searching for someone to share their hobby with.

Workshops are also popular with singles. You can take workshops on subjects such as developing relationships, building self-esteem, gaining financial independence, and selling real estate. College and adult education courses and workshops offer plenty of opportunities for single people to meet and develop relationships based on shared interests, goals, and backgrounds. Furthermore, studying together can be so enjoyable!

Lines for College and Adult Education Courses and Workshops

☐ "What made you decide to take this course/workshop?"

☐ "How long have you been interested in this subject?"

☐ "If you need a study partner, I'd certainly be willing to volunteer."

☐ "Do you mind if I look at your notes?"

LECTURES

Lectures, either in a college setting or in other places, are another ideal way to meet single prospects. Lectures on a variety of subjects are publicized in college and local newspapers, on radio, and on television.

If the subject of a particular lecture interests you, be sure to attend the lecture and keep your eyes open for attractive singles. During a break in the lecture, during the question and answer session, or at refreshment time, strike up a conversation with a prospect. Prospects can be attending the lecture or working at the hall.

Remember that you can attend college lectures even if you've been out of college for years or never went to college. But do have a genuine interest in the subject being discussed, so that you sound somewhat knowledgeable when you strike up a conversation with an exciting prospect.

Lines for Lectures

- ☐ "How long have you been interested in this subject?"
- ☐ "Have you done any other reading/research/studying on this subject?"
- ☐ "What did you think of this lecture/lecturer?"
- ☐ "This lecture was on one of my favorite subjects."
- ☐ "Have you ever been to the museum? It has an incredible collection of related items, memorabilia, and information on this subject."

SCHOOL MEETINGS AND EVENTS

If you are a single parent—and the world is full of them—try to attend as many Parent-Teacher Association (PTA) meetings as possible at your child's school. Besides receiving important information about the school, its curriculum, and its problems, you will also meet and interact with many other single parents, as well as single teachers. One of those single parents or teachers might be very happy that you decided to attend that meeting.

In addition to PTA meetings, many other events are staples in the school calendar. Is your child in a play? In the orchestra or band? On the football team? How many children in these groups have single parents watching them perform? Also leave room in your schedule for the carnivals, learning fairs, and other events that your child either is participating in or would just like to attend in your company.

If you don't have a child of your own, try to "borrow" one. Is your sister or brother too busy to take your niece or nephew to the May Day Fair? Is your neighbor's child helping out at the Fifth Grade Car Wash? Use your imagination. As many parents are quick to point out, when you have children, your circle of friends enlarges a hundredfold.

Lines for School Meetings and Events

☐ "Who are your child's teachers?"

☐ "Do you ever wish you were back in school again?"

☐ "Do your children get a lot of homework?"

☐ "I can't believe how much these desks have shrunk!"

☐ "Did you go to ____? You look very familiar."
(*Insert name of school.*)

SINGLE PARENT CLUBS

Single parent clubs offer an opportunity for single, divorced, or widowed parents to meet and connect with each other. These clubs are everywhere and include single parents of all ages. Many of these clubs are affiliated with a church or religious organization.

If you are a single parent, be sure to join a single parent club in your area. An example is Parents Without Partners. These clubs generally hold meetings on a regular basis, as well as sponsoring mixers, outings, and other social events. In addition to meeting prospects, you can become friends with people of either sex with similar family situations and problems.

Lines for Single Parent Clubs

☐ "Where do your children go to school?"

☐ "Who is your child's pediatrician?"

☐ "How do you deal with your child when he/she talks back/throws a tantrum/misses curfew?"

CAT, DOG, AND HORSE SHOWS

There are many ways that pets can help you to meet prospects. One unusual way is to go to a show featuring your favorite type of animal.

For example, at a cat show, you'll find throngs of single feline fanciers. Cats make wonderful pets and require only a small amount of daily maintenance. Often, a single person's lifestyle does not provide the freedom to attend to a pet's needs, especially during the workday. A cat does not have to be walked every few hours. Add to that the beauty, gracefulness, and companionship that a cat provides, and you've got a winning pet for a single person.

Cat shows bring all types of breeds under one roof. They also bring out cat-loving singles, as well as breeders and groomers who are single. Purr on over to an exciting prospect.

Dogs are man's—and woman's—best friend, and people just love them. Some people love their dogs so much that they want to groom them and show them off at area dog shows. Dog shows display canines of all sizes, shapes, and breeds. They generally teem with single people raving over a variety of dogs. If you're a dog lover, or just an animal lover in general, dog shows are an ideal spot to meet attractive singles out for a fun time.

Single horse lovers should make it a point to attend horse shows. Attractive single prospects can usually be found either appreciating the horses or proudly displaying them. There's no law against looking at a beautiful horse and simultaneously eyeing its attractive single owner or groomer! Trot on over and make your move.

Lines for Cat, Dog, and Horse Shows

☐ "Do you have a cat/dog/horse?"

☐ "What's your favorite breed?"

☐ "When I was a kid, I always wanted a cat/dog, but our mailman was terrified of them, so my mother wouldn't let me have one."

☐ "I have a crazy dog. He has a fear of being bitten by our mailman."

☐ "The only thing about cats that I don't like is cleaning the litter box. I guess I just don't do litter boxes—but I do, do lunch. Would you care to join me for some?"

☐ "If you're going to flash that blue ribbon smile at me, don't you think you ought to know my name?"

☐ "You have to meet my cat/dog/horse. He'd love you."

☐ "My cat/dog/horse would love you, and he's very selective."

HORSEBACK RIDING CLUBS

Whether you own a horse or are just a horseback riding enthusiast, another way to meet single prospects is to join a horseback riding club. Horseback riding clubs offer members an opportunity to share the thrills and joys of horseback riding and to go on fascinating excursions. Rides are planned for all times of the day, so just about any schedule can be met. Single prospects can be found as club members, trainers, groomers, horse owners, stable investors, or staff members, all of whom have that one strong love of horses and horseback riding as the common bond.

One way to meet other single prospects through a horseback riding club is to get to the stable about fifteen to thirty minutes before the scheduled time and mingle with the other members. If you find a prospect you're interested in, you can canter together during the ride.

To join a horseback riding club, contact local stables and academies, which are listed in the Yellow Pages. Look in the sports section of your local newspaper for a listing of horse shows and the names of the stables, academies, or clubs sponsoring them. Horse or equestrian magazines, found in bookstores and on newsstands, may also provide leads.

Lines for Horseback Riding Clubs

☐ "How long have you been horseback riding?"

☐ "That's a beautiful horse. What's his name?"

☐ "That horse has a very pleasant disposition. Did you just feed him? That's the way I am, too—feed me and I suddenly become pleasant."

FITNESS CENTERS

The idea with fitness centers is to throw on some stylish fitness wear and get into shape. In addition to tightening up your body, you have a chance to meet other singles. Also, what you see is what you get, so there should be no surprises or disappointments with the prospects you meet.

At one time, co-ed fitness centers, gyms, and workout clinics were a prime location for singles to meet and mingle. People now, however, are more conscientious about getting and keeping themselves in shape and go to fitness centers for the sole purpose of working out. Nevertheless, fitness centers are still a viable alternative for connecting with the opposite sex.

If you enjoy aerobics, co-ed aerobics classes may be just the ticket for you. Put on your exercise outfit, go to a class, and get a wonderful cardiovascular workout. Pick a spot near an attractive prospect; this way you can make small talk while exercising or when finished. You can discuss the workout, the instructor, physical fitness, your prospect's outfit, or any other topic of interest.

Lines for Fitness Centers

☐ "I'm exhausted. Do you know CPR in case I collapse?"

☐ "Would you join me in an aerobic sprint to the juice bar for a drink?"

☐ "You're an excellent example of someone who exercises. Generally, the only exercise I get is in the summertime when bees chase me to and from my car."

☐ "If I told you that your body was gorgeous, would you hold it against me?"

☐ "Just looking at you has rejuvenated all the cells in my body. I want to thank you, and all of my cells thank you."

YOGA AND TRANSCENDENTAL MEDITATION CLASSES

Another way to meet interesting singles is to attend yoga or transcendental meditation (TM) classes. Yoga and TM are techniques used as a means of finding peace and tranquility within yourself. They can be ideal for singles who live turbulent, fast-paced, stressed-out lives. They also help you to become balanced by bringing you into harmony with nature and with the world around you.

By exploring your inner self through yoga or TM, you have the potential to become a better person. That alone should aid you in attracting and meeting other quality singles. In addition, once again, you're meeting people at these classes who share an interest with you, which may make them more receptive to developing a friendship or even a relationship.

Lines for Yoga and Transcendental Meditation Classes

☐ "I need yoga/TM to calm my heart after gazing at you."

☐ "How did you first become interested in yoga/TM?"

☐ "My heart is in yoga/TM, but my legs are putting up a little fuss."
(*This line is for use when getting into or out of the yoga posture.*)

SUPPORT GROUPS

If you are a member of a support group, you know how valuable the help and advice they offer can be. But have you thought of looking at your support group as a source of prospects, too? In the members of your support group, you have people who share your particular problem, understand what you are going through, and can offer sound advice from personal experience. Making closer contact with a single member from your group will not only bring you additional support in times of stress but also companionship for more lighthearted moments.

If you are single, have any kind of problem, and do not belong to a support group, remember that there is emotional support available for you, along with a good opportunity to meet single prospects in a comparable situation. Support groups are available for almost every type of problem, from weight disorders and shyness to alcoholism and debilitating diseases such as cancer, diabetes, heart disease, and arthritis. Support groups are also available for the relatives and friends of people with serious problems.

Lines for Support Groups

☐ "How long have you been a member of this group?"

☐ "Would you like to go for a cup of coffee after the meeting?"

☐ "Will you be here next week?"

☐ "I like your voice. It's really soothing."

☐ "You have a pretty smile. It really makes me feel good when I see you smile."

FAN CLUBS AND CONVENTIONS

Star Trek and other popular television shows have spawned fan clubs and science fiction conventions around the country and the world. Fans of these shows can join clubs to receive newsletters or "fanzines," memorabilia, and news of upcoming events such as autograph parties and conventions. The conventions are often held in huge auditoriums or arenas and draw thousands of the faithful. You don't need to be a member of a club to attend a convention, however. Conventions are open to the public and draw hundreds of the mildly interested and just curious, too.

But if you're a Trekkie or a serious fan of another show, you should consider joining the fan club. The television show that caused the creation of the club might fade into boob tube heaven someday, but maybe you'll have found someone to watch your old tapes with. Regular meetings are generally not part of fan club agendas, but local members may meet occasionally for lunch or cocktails. Some clubs also feature pen pal services.

Television shows are not the only things that attract fans. Many musical performers brag of fan club followings, as do a numbers of actors, actresses, athletes, sports teams, and the like.

Lines for Fan Clubs and Science Fiction Conventions

☐ "Do you know where the Gilligan's Island booth is? Only kidding."
(This line to be said with humor.)

☐ "Do you know when _____'s next concert is, and would you like to go?"
(Insert name of star.)

☐ "Do you think the rumors about _____ are true?"
(Insert name of star.)
— *(Reply)* "What rumors?"
— "_____ wants us very much to meet."

☐ "Who's your favorite character on this show?"

☐ "What do you think was the best _____ episode?"
(Insert name of show.)

☐ "You won't believe this, but I just saw two people get beamed up in the restroom. Have you also noticed anything funny going on?"

☐ "I would like to thank the powers that be for beaming your molecules into my path."

☐ "Are we bonding or is this just an unexpectedly pleasant cosmic encounter?"

☐ "I didn't think they grew anyone on this planet that looked as good as you."

18. Indoor Meeting Places

*I*f the weather is not conducive to outdoor activities, don't despair. There are many things you can do indoors to meet singles. Although the possibilities are limited only by your imagination, we'll discuss just three examples—houses of worship, laundromats, and libraries. We'll also take a look at such indoor standbys as professional office waiting rooms and long lines in facilities such as banks and post offices.

HOUSES OF WORSHIP

Go to your chosen house of faith on your day of worship, and you might be amazed at all the single prospects you'll find. Many single people have some religious beliefs and enjoy attending church or synagogue. While you're being seated, or while the sermon is progressing, scan the congregation for attractive prospects. When you find someone that you are attracted to, "lock on" to him or her with eye contact and a smile. You can make your initial move right after the sermon or service is over, or during an intermission period.

In addition to prayer services, many churches and synagogues are the settings for a variety of religious clubs, classes, and other activities. These functions are also ideal for meeting prospects.

If you're waiting at home, praying to meet someone, and getting no results, you should try your local church or synagogue. Your prayers just may be answered there.

Lines for Houses of Worship

☐ "My inner voice said that I should come to church/synagogue today, and I'm glad I listened."

☐ "You look like the answer to my prayers."

☐ "I honestly hope this is divine fate that I am lucky enough to meet you like this."

☐ "Just checking to see if you were made in heaven."
(*This line should be said while checking the tag at the back of your prospect's collar.*)

LAUNDROMATS

Another place to meet single prospects is, strange as it may seem, the laundromat. Many singles live in apartments or houses that don't have a washer or dryer. They therefore spend at least some time every week, usually on Saturday or Sunday, in the laundromat. While their clothes are rinsing and spin drying, these singles usually read a book or magazine out of boredom.

Laundromats offer various opportunities to begin a conversation. Break the ice with a prospect while loading or unloading your clothes, adding detergent or fabric softener to your washer, getting quarters from the change machine, or simply waiting for your machine to finish. Many laundromats now have televisions for the patrons to watch while waiting; these provide many topics to help start conversations. Some laundromats even feature "singles nights," where you'll find music, dancing, beer, food, roses, and a hostess to coordinate different activities. "Singles nights" are usually held by savvy entrepreneurs on the slowest night of the week for regular business. Of course, there will still be loads of singles with piles of dirty clothes to be washed on any night of the week! Whichever way you look at it, if you use laundromats to do your wash, you should seriously consider the potential of meeting prospects there.

Lines for Laundromats

☐ "What are the advantages of your detergent over mine?"

☐ "Can I give you a hand with that load?"

☐ "Which machines would you recommend?"

☐ "Would you care to take a spin during the spin cycle?"

☐ "I've been thinking about trying your detergent. Have you ever used mine?"

☐ "Can I get you some more change while you load your washer/ dryer?"

☐ "I found this sock on the floor. Is it yours?"

☐ "Could I borrow a cup of bleach/a dryer sheet?"

☐ "Would you like some help folding your clothes?"

☐ "Would you like to go for ____ during the drying cycle?" (*Insert appropriate beverage.*)

☐ "I've never used fabric softener. Is it really worth using?"

☐ "I feel like I've aged ten years while waiting for my clothes to dry."

☐ "When I came in here to wash my clothes, I was cleanly shaved—and look at me now."
(*This line is for use by a man with whiskers.*)

☐ "I've got two dryers here, but I only need one. Would you like to use the second?"

LIBRARIES

The library is a marvelous place to meet someone new. You can start a conversation over any subject that you or your prospect may be reading about. Some places where you can look for singles are among the stacks, at the worktables, by the magazine stands, and by the video tape racks. Another great place is by the card catalog, where it is easy and stress-free to ask someone a question about library procedure. Many successful relationships have begun in libraries, with a love of reading or an interest in a specific subject as the common denominator.

Lines for Libraries

☐ "Could you help me look up something in the card catalog?"

☐ "Have you read any good books recently?"

☐ "Do you know anything about the latest releases?"

☐ "Where are the ___?"
(*Insert type of book.*)

PROFESSIONAL OFFICE WAITING ROOMS

As strange as it may seem, you can meet prospects while waiting to see your doctor, dentist, lawyer, or other professional. It's true that some people in waiting rooms sit with their heads down, waiting (anonymously, hopefully, fearfully) for their name to be called. But there are other people who, to make the time go by, are very willing to make conversation.

Lines for Professional Office Waiting Rooms

☐ "Have you been waiting here long?"

☐ "What have you heard about this ____?"
(*Insert appropriate type of professional.*)

☐ "When I first showed up for my appointment, I was fourteen years old!"

☐ "Isn't this a beautiful/noisy/interesting waiting room?"

☐ "You have the most beautiful eye."
(*This humorous line is for use in an optometrist's or optician's waiting room.*)

LONG LINES

Any time you have to stand on a long line (for example, at the Department of Motor Vehicles, the post office, or the bank), look at it as a great, although unusual, place to meet singles. People tend to respond more willingly to opening lines or questions when they're waiting on line. After all, while waiting on line, there isn't very much to do, except chit chat. So, when you are ready to get on line, look around first. If your timing is good, you can position yourself directly behind a good prospect on the same line or beside one on the next line. Then don't wait; make your move!

Lines for Long Lines

☐ "How long have you been waiting?"

☐ "What type of car do you drive?"
(*This line is for use at the Department of Motor Vehicles.*)

☐ "Is this where I get a license for my horse?"
(*This line is for use at the Department of Motor Vehicles.*)

☐ "I hope this bank doesn't run out of money by the time we get up to a teller!"

☐ "My license/registration will expire by the time I get up to the counter."

☐ "If they had to pay us to wait in line, we'd be out of here a lot faster!"

19. Shopping

S hopping is one of those activities that everyone must do at one time or another. But instead of letting it be a chore, why not make it pleasurable and productive? After all, you're not the only single person shopping—why not try to meet some prospects? Let's discuss some of the places where most people shop regularly and what you can do to meet other singles there.

SUPERMARKETS

Shopping in a supermarket is a terrific way to meet prospects. You can scan the aisles for an attractive prospect and then, when the prospect strolls into your immediate vicinity, put on your most perplexed look and ask a contrived question about a product: "Do you know what the difference is between pea pods and peas?" "Do you know what shelf the canned unsweetened turnips are on?" It doesn't matter if your product question is genuine or ridiculously absurd. What matters is that you make contact.

Also, in a supermarket, if you get a smile or glance from a prospect, there are a multitude of aisles, in addition to the checkout counters, where you can make follow-up contact. Use the angled mirrors on the ceiling to keep track of your prospect's movements.

Lines for Supermarkets

☐ "May I push your cart? I'm the local pusher."

☐ "Did you get everything on your shopping list?"

☐ "Excuse me, but I'd like to cite you for double-parking your shopping cart in aisle five."

☐ "Two thousand carts outside and I pick the one with a squeaky wheel. Do you have any oil on you?"

☐ "May I have the honor of double-bagging for you?"

☐ "Do you think we'll make it to the front of the line while we still have a few good years left?"

☐ "Thank you for your road courtesy. You're a good driver." (*This line is for use with a prospect who has moved his or her shopping cart in some way to let you pass.*)

☐ "That looks like a serious load."

☐ "Decisions, decisions—should I choose the long checkout line with the light loads, or should I go with the short line of heavy loads? Why is life so troubling?"

☐ "Please, no speeding. We use radar to catch speeders in these aisles." (*This line is for use with a prospect who is moving briskly down the aisle with a shopping cart.*)

HEALTH FOOD STORES

Health food stores are great places to meet attractive, health-conscious prospects. Many singles spend their spare time working out to get and stay in optimum shape. These singles tend to also shop at health food stores for protein or diet shakes, vitamin supplements, cruelty-free cosmetics, and healthy foods. People who shop in health food stores care about their health and about the environment. What better quality could you want in a prospect than respect for good health and for the Earth?

Lines for Health Food Stores

☐ "Do you know if I can get organic vegetables or fruit here?"

☐ "I'm looking for an effective weight-loss product. What do you use to stay so trim?"

☐ "I've been told that if I eat outdated yogurt and take vitamins beyond their expiration date that I could be inadvertently beamed into a time warp. Do you know anything about that?"

☐ "What vitamins do you take to look so healthy?"

☐ "You must take a lot of vitamins to look that beautiful/handsome."

SHOPPING MALLS

Shopping malls are excellent places to meet prospects. Malls are loaded with single people out spending money or just window-shopping. Prospects can be found walking in and out of stores, browsing, snacking in the food court, or sitting on benches relaxing. Just be casual, friendly, and sincere in your approach. Remember, there's no reason you can't buy a pair of shoes on sale plus meet a prospect in the same afternoon.

Lines for Shopping Malls

☐ "What's your favorite store in this mall?"

☐ "Are there any good sales here today?"

☐ "I want you to know that you've been the best part of my shopping experience."

☐ "If you're hedging on whether to buy that ____, let me say that you'd look wonderful in it."
(*Insert appropriate article of clothing. This line is for use with clothing shoppers only.*)

☐ "So, what are you buying for me? You don't have to keep it a secret. You can tell me now."

☐ "Do you have change of a dollar?"

DEPARTMENT STORES

Department stores are another good source of single people. You've got a lot of prospects browsing through the various departments, while more are working throughout the store. Go department-store shopping before or after any major holiday, but be careful because you could get whiplash from scanning the countless prospects whisking through their shopping or work activities.

Try to meet as many prospects as possible. Some astute singles are already aware of this prospecting bonanza, and now you can join their ranks.

Lines for Department Stores

☐ "How does this look on me?"

☐ "What do you think of this as a gift for my ____?"
(*Insert name of friend or relative.*)

☐ "Do you know where to find men's clothing/customer service/the elevator?"

☐ "I was thinking of getting this perfume for my mother/cologne for my father. What do you think of the scent?"

☐ "I'd like to get a real nice shirt/a comfortable pair of slippers/a functional but elegant lamp. Do you have any suggestions?"

☐ "I was thinking about getting a giant-screen television. Do you know which makes are the most reliable and have the best picture quality?"

☐ "If I purchase a stereo VCR, do I have to get a stereo television?"

☐ "Do you know how many extra speakers I would need to make my television sound surround me?"

AUTOMOTIVE STORES

Probably the best specialty store a woman could "shop at" to meet single men is an automotive store. Many single men spend hours working on their cars, or fixing up old cars, as a hobby. They will be impressed by a woman looking at distributor caps or even just at steering wheel covers. Most will be more than happy to answer any questions. Look for prospects entering or leaving the store, browsing in the aisles, milling in front of the store, or working behind the counters. Just have some knowledge about the auto part you're supposedly looking for, and you may leave the store with a part you don't know what to do with but with a date for Friday night.

Lines for Automotive Stores

☐ "I was thinking about getting sheepskin seat covers for my car. Do you know how to put them on bucket seats/a bench seat?"

☐ "Should I get a pair of snow tires for the winter, or am I better off with a set of all-season radials?"

☐ "I need new windshield wipers for my car. Are they difficult to install? Do you know how to put them on?"

☐ "I'm getting windshield washer fluid for my car but I don't know where to pour it in. Would you have a minute to show me?"

☐ "My map light/overhead light flickers on and off. Could you tell me where the replacement bulbs are and how to put them in?"

SWAP MEETS AND FLEA MARKETS

Swap meets and flea markets are always great places for meeting prospects. Most people are happy and at ease there, making it a good environment to strike up a conversation. A little eye contact, a smile, and you're on your way. Conversation can be started easily over interests such as antiques, collectibles, or bargains. You can converse about how ecstatic you are not having to be at work, or about how you really like being able to trade or swap for something you want, instead of having to spend cash. Whatever comes to mind to begin a friendly conversation is enough to initiate contact. Then offer to treat your new acquaintance to lunch, an ice-cream cone, or a cup of coffee.

Lines for Swap Meets and Flea Markets

☐ "I shop here regularly. How come I haven't seen you before?"

☐ "The only part about shopping that I hate is carrying all those heavy bags from the car into the house."

☐ "I hope you've found what you were looking for." *If the answer is no:* "Well, then let me be of assistance to you. *If the answer is yes:* "You must be a good shopper. Maybe you could help me find what I'm looking for."

YARD AND HOUSE SALES

Many homeowners and apartment dwellers sell unwanted belongings at advertised yard or house sales. Singles looking to furnish or accessorize their houses or apartments inexpensively often shop at these events for bargains. You can, too, but keep your eyes open for appealing prospects as well.

Lines for Yard and House Sales

☐ "I need to get a birthday gift for my ____. You look like you have good taste. Do you have any suggestions?" (*Insert name of friend or relative.*)

☐ "Do you think this table could be successfully stripped and stained?"

☐ "Look at this! Do you think it could be worth something?"

FARMERS MARKETS

Farmers markets frequently house many different vendors under one roof. You're likely to find singles meandering about searching for fresh vegetables, fruit, bread, pastries, meat, fish, gourmet snacks, flowers, or something similar. Most farmers markets allow only vendors who carry fresh, high quality products. Stop in at a local farmers market and treat your palate to some new taste sensations. Also, treat your eyes to some fine-looking prospects.

Lines for Farmers Markets

☐ "Is the produce fresh today?"

☐ "I just love fresh fruits and vegetables. How about you?"

☐ "When I see these fresh foods, I just want to go out and grow them myself."

CARD SHOPS

How can card shops be helpful to you? In some busy ones, you'll find prospects chuckling over card selections up and down the aisles. Once you spot an attractive prospect, position yourself near him or her and act like you're looking for a card. It will be much easier to strike up a conversation if you're both looking at the same kind of cards. With a little luck, you will need to return to the card shop to buy an affection card for your newfound friend.

Lines for Card Shops

☐ "What do you think of this card for my ____?"
(*Insert name of friend or relative.*)

☐ "Do you like funny cards, or do you prefer the more serious ones?"

☐ "Excuse me, but can I help you find a card? I don't work here, but I'd just love to help you."

BOOKSTORES AND RECORD STORES

Other shops where singles abound are bookstores and record stores. People love reading, and you are apt to find a lot of prospects standing in the aisles browsing through books. The best time to scan bookstores for single prospects is on weekends, as most people are off from work. However, with the advent of the mega-bookstores such as Borders or Barnes and Noble, many of which now feature chic espresso bars, more and more singles can be found meandering through the aisles or sipping capuccino on weekdays, too.

Record stores are also popular with singles. Look in the section featuring the type of music you prefer, and you'll have a ready-made shared interest. But if the prospect is really appealing to you, forget the music—just hum a hello. You can take turns with the stereo, when the time comes.

Lines for Bookstores and Record Stores

- [ ] "Do you know where the ____ are?"
  (*Insert type of book, record, or tape.*)

- [ ] "Can you tell me where I can find ____?"
  (*Insert type of book, record, or tape.*)

- [ ] "What kind of books/music do you like?"

- [ ] "I have a huge cassette collection. Do you think it would be ridiculous to get a compact disc player and start collecting CD's now?"

- [ ] "What do you think of this book/cassette?"

VIDEO STORES

Considering the cost and effort involved in going out to the movies, many singles are finding it much simpler and cheaper to rent a movie and watch it at home. If your town or neighborhood has one of the big chain video stores such as West Coast Video or Blockbuster Video, the odds will be better that you'll meet prospects, since these stores usually have a larger selection of movie titles and more copies of each title to enable them to service a more substantial clientele. If a small video store is all that you have, however, so be it; single people go there, too. Just keep your eyes on the door as much as on the movie boxes.

You can find prospects wandering about the different aisles deciding which movies to rent or at the service counter renting or returning tapes.

Lines for Video Stores

☐ "Do you know anything about this movie?"

☐ "I'm looking for a good comedy/thriller/mystery. Have you seen any good ones you could recommend?"

☐ "How long have you been a member here?"

CASHIERS

Prospects, as mentioned throughout Part II of this book, are found not just attending functions or visiting sites but also working at them. Cashiers are an example. Every store you go into will have a cashier. Every function or site you visit where you have to pay will also have a cashier or the equivalent. So, the next time you reach into your wallet to pay for something, remember that you may also have a chance to walk away with a date for lunch or a movie.

Lines for Cashiers

☐ "You impress me with the way you handle money. What do you think about mutual funds?"

☐ "Could you please try to keep the total down for me?"
(*This line often works very well. Since a product costs what it costs, the cashier will usually chuckle.*)

☐ "Don't forget my ten-percent senior citizen's discount."
(*This line works well when you're anything but a senior citizen and your prospect knows it.*)

☐ "Price check—aisle four! I don't know why (maybe I need to be committed to an institution), but I've always wanted to say that in a supermarket checkout line."

20. Transportation

*P*eople have to travel. And what's wrong with trying to strike up a conversation with someone interesting while you're getting from one place to another? One of the reasons travel is so conducive to meeting prospects is that, for a period of time, you and your fellow travelers are confined to the vehicle of transportation. There are some people who are so successful at meeting prospects while traveling that they go on short bus or train trips specifically for the purpose. At their destination, they just turn around and go right back home again. So, consider using your transit time to approach interesting prospects the next time you have to travel.

TRAINS, BUSES, AND STATIONS

Many singles use the bus or train on a daily basis to commute to work or school. Chances are that if you are one of these people, you see attractive prospects every day either on your way to or returning home from your day's activities. You don't need to be a regular commuter, however, to take advantage of the opportunities on the train or bus. If you need to travel for any reason, keep your eyes and ears open. You can make contact in the ticket office, on the platform while waiting for your train or bus, on the train or bus, or even when leaving the train or bus. In addition, if you're waiting for a friend or relative to arrive, be sure to scan the platform and pick a good spot to do your waiting in.

Lines for Trains, Buses, and Stations

☐ "Would you join me for the ride in/home?"

☐ "I don't know what it is, but whenever I have an important meeting/a must-make appointment/a crucial exam, the train/bus is invariably late."

☐ "That looks like an interesting book. What's it about?"

☐ "Can I buy you ____ while we wait?"
(*Insert appropriate beverage.*)

☐ "I've been taking this train/bus to work/school for a long time, and I can't believe I've never seen you."

☐ "I will give you personalized shuttle-bus service to any place on the planet that you desire. Just point me in your favorite direction."
(*This line is for use on a bus or at a bus station.*)

AIRPLANES AND AIRPORTS

Airplanes and airports also offer great opportunities to meet other singles. Many people take planes for business reasons, for vacations, or to visit friends or relatives. Single prospects can be found working on the plane or in the terminal, standing in line at the check-in counter, killing time in the gift shop or restaurant, waiting at the gate, sitting on the plane, waiting for their luggage in the baggage claim area, or waiting for a taxi, limo, or shuttlebus. Also watch for singles who are waiting for or dropping off a traveler. The opportunities abound for meeting prospects at the airport or on a plane. So the next time someone asks you for a lift to the airport, say yes.

Lines for Airplanes and Airports

☐ "Would you like some help carrying your luggage?"

☐ "The instant I saw you, I realized it wasn't important if I was departing or arriving. I only wanted to meet this lovely/handsome person."

☐ "You even look good with an oxygen mask strapped over your face."
(*This line is for use with the flight attendant after he/she demonstrates how to use the oxygen mask.*)

☐ "Excuse me. Are you a (*name of airline*) flight attendant? I'm flying (*name of airline*), and I hope the attendants on my flight look as good as you."

☐ "I want to thank the ticket agent. He/she promised me that there would be a beautiful girl/handsome man on this flight, and he/she didn't lie."

AUTOMOBILES

Difficult as it may be to believe, you can also meet prospects while you are either driving in a car or pulled up at a traffic light or stop sign. Now, this technique is not recommended for everyone, but it does work. And of course, at all times, you must be sure that you're in total control of your vehicle, so that you don't jeopardize your safety or that of your passengers, prospect, or anyone else.

Initially, you might be either driving along or pulled up at a light or stop sign and notice an attractive prospect in the car in the next lane. Often, people waiting at red lights or stop signs, or even busy driving, will glance at the cars on either side of them. At the appropriate moment, make eye contact and flash your pearly whites. If your prospect is at all interested, you should get a reciprocal, inviting smile. Unfortunately, whether or not your prospect is interested, the light will turn green or the traffic will clear from the stop sign, and your prospect will refocus on the road and pull away. So how do you meet this attractive prospect who is driving out of your life?

When trying to connect with a prospect while you are both driving, you must make eye contact and get either a reciprocal smile or some other positive acknowledgement of your being. Assuming at least one of these prerequisites has been met, you should now attempt to meet your prospect.

The first place you can probably make initial contact is at the next light or stop sign. Follow your prospect but stay in an adjoining lane to make it easier to pull up alongside the prospect when you both come to a stop. Just keep in mind that time is of the essence. You have only about a minute at the most to make a connection and develop a rapport. You must make your move quickly. Roll down your window, give your horn a light beep to get your prospect's attention, and make a motion for your prospect to lower his or her window. Your prospect, of course, will have absolutely no idea of what you want at this point; he or she may think that you need directions. This is when you should blow the prospect away with a creative ice-breaker.

Flatter your prospect immediately, and try to get a laugh or a smile. Identify yourself by your first name. Ask your prospect for his or her phone number, and assure the prospect that you will call. If your prospect won't give you his or her phone number but instead asks for yours, you'll have no choice but to comply. Obviously, that's a bad sign, but it's not a complete negative. Bear in mind that in these times, most people are cautious. Many people won't give their number to a total stranger, but there's always a chance that your prospect will. And if you give your number out, there's always a chance that your prospect will call you. What do you have to lose?

Also, when you are pulled up at a traffic light or stop sign, you can make a gesture or verbal suggestion to pull over at the next restaurant, convenience store, gas station, or other stopping place to meet and talk. (You might even hold up a sign, prepared in advance, that says that you'd like to pull over and say hello.) There are times when taking charge like this works effectively.

A typical scenario with a positive connection in an automobile might go as follows: Your prospect rolls down his or her car window at a stoplight in response to your effort to make contact.

You: You have a beautiful smile, and I just can't let you drive out of my life without getting your name and phone number. My name is ___, and I promise I'll call you. (*Insert your first name.*)

Prospect: But I don't know you!

You: That's why I want your phone number, especially before the light changes. Then I can call you, and we can get to know one another.

Prospect: Okay, my number is 555–1234.

You: 555–1234, you've made my day! I promise I'll call you. Drive safely!

You may not have a choice about the car that you're driving, and any average car really will do, but it won't hurt your cause if you drive a convertible, sports car, exotic car, classic car, or any vehicle that generally draws positive response from other drivers. Conversely, any vehicle that could be classified as an eyesore or obnoxious will hinder your potential to meet prospects while driving.

Lines for Automobiles

☐ "This may sound terribly forward, but I didn't want you to drive away without my getting your name and phone number."

☐ "I just can't let you drive out of my life without getting your name and phone number. My name is ____, and I promise I'll call you."
(Insert first name.)

☐ "My only wish in life is to speak with you on this phone/your phone."
(*This line is for use if either you or your prospect has a car telephone.*)

☐ "I've been thinking about buying a car just like yours. How do you like it?"

TRAFFIC JAMS

Another place to connect with single prospects is in a traffic jam. A traffic jam could be the result of rush hour, a bridge opening, a traffic accident, road construction, or a similar hair-pulling situation. Sometimes, when traffic is bottled up and going nowhere, people get out of their cars to stretch their legs, mingle, and chat. So, the next time you're stuck in a traffic jam, calm down, turn off your radio, and check the cars around you for appealing prospects. Remember what they say: You can turn lemons into lemonade!

Lines for Traffic Jams

☐ "Can you believe this traffic?"

☐ "Doesn't it always seem like you get stuck in traffic when you're in a hurry?"

☐ "We have to stop meeting like this."

☐ "Well, I may hate getting stuck in traffic, but at least it gives me the opportunity to talk with you."

☐ "How did a nice person like you get stuck in a traffic jam like this?"

21. Singles Dating Clubs and Video Dating Services

S ome people join a singles dating club or video dating service to get "professional" help with their dating search. Others feel frustrated in their personal search and hope that these services can provide the names and phone numbers that they have been unable to get on their own. Singles dating clubs and video dating services are not for everyone, however. While some singles like the precise, high-tech methods used, others feel that microchips and video tapes take the romance out of dating. You need to decide for yourself if a computerized approach is for you.

Singles dating clubs and video dating services are basically the same. Both offer you the opportunity to meet other members who have been matched up with you according to comprehensive physical and psychological profiles. Depending on your budget, a membership or renewal can be very costly, though, and may net you only a few telephone numbers. On top of this, some of the numbers may be for people who reside too far away from you to make a dating relationship feasible.

Video dating services go one step beyond singles dating clubs. In addition to using a computer to match you up with other members, video dating services also give you an opportunity to view firsthand what your prospects look like. The service is often expensive, but wouldn't it be worthwhile if you met your mate for life on one of those videos?

One firm that has had considerable success with its video dating program is Great Expectations. It has various dating programs available, but its standard "until married" membership is the most popular. Great Expectations offers members the freedom to make their own selections, whereas many other video dating services do the selecting for members. By making your own selections, you are in total control of who you meet, and at the same time, you remain anonymous until a selection is made.

At Great Expectations, the selection process starts by reviewing alphabetical listings of members, segregated by sex. Typed profiles and photographs of the members are kept in A-through-Z looseleaf binders. All the members are identified by their first names and membership codes only, which are cross-referenced to their videos. It may take several office visits to go through all of the notebooks and to select the videos you wish to view.

The video profiles on the members are short but sweet. From the five-minute video, you should be able to decide if you have any further interest in a member. If you are interested, Great Expectations will send a postcard to the member indicating that another member would like to meet him or her. The selected member can then visit the Great Expectations office to examine your typed profile and video. If the member you chose is interested in you, too, Great Expectations will then give him or her your phone number to initiate contact. If the member you selected is not interested in you, you would not be contacted.

If you're single but unable to afford a dating service, you should consider getting a part- or full-time sales, marketing, or clerical job with a dating firm. Not only would you put money in your pocket, but you would also be exposed to genuine and sincere prospects while in your work environment. Also, if you wished to join the dating service, you would probably get an employee's discount off the normal membership or application fee!

With or without a discount, the membership fees for singles dating clubs and video dating services can be hefty. With this in mind, try to get a list of satisfied customers from the club or service you'd like to join, then phone some of the listed members and ask them about their experiences and success. You might also call your local Better Business Bureau or Chamber of Commerce to verify that the club or service is legitimate and a quality enterprise. Ask your friends, too, if they know anyone who has ever belonged.

Before we leave the subject of video dating, let's quickly discuss the popular television show *Love Connection*, which has successfully introduced hundreds of happy couples. Several spinoffs of *Love Connection* can also be found on the tube. You may want to sign up to appear on *Love Connection*. Although it's taped primarily in California, it does travel to different parts of the country on occasion. The catch? Whether your evening out was good or bad, you and your date must report back to the show a few weeks later and discuss your experience. Of course, your adventure will be recapped in front of millions of viewers. If you're a private person, this may not be for you. Otherwise, *Love Connection* could be a sensational way for you to find the "love-of-your-life connection."

22. Personal Ads

*P*ersonal ads are currently one of the hottest ways, if not *the* hottest way, to meet prospects. Why? Because any time you try to meet other people, you're "selling" yourself, and some people feel very uncomfortable "selling" themselves in a face-to-face manner. Many people feel that physical attributes have become too much of a priority in today's society. But that doesn't mean that the only people who use "the personals" are physically deficient! There are many good-looking, intelligent people who place or respond to ads, some because they're too busy to go out as often as they feel they would need to and others because they want to get to know a prospect before they go on a date.

In this chapter, we'll discuss both placing personal ads and responding to them. But first, let's discuss how to get started.

GETTING STARTED

The first step in using personal ads is to identify the local newspapers and magazines that run ads for singles. Make sure that you like the way the ads are displayed and the procedures that are used to place or respond to them. Once you have decided which periodical you want to use, you should decide whether you prefer drawing up your own ad or responding to someone else's. Responding to ads is simple and will get you started inexpensively. (Responding to ads will be covered later in this chapter.) Many people, however, find that it is more productive to write and place their own ads.

WRITING YOUR OWN AD

Personal ads take time and effort to write and money to place. However, instead of waiting for a reply from ads you have responded to, if you place your own ad, you will be exposed to hundreds, possibly thousands, of singles. If your ad is written well, even a one-time placement may bring you dozens of replies, if not more. One of the advantages of writing your own ad is that you are in the position of choosing whom to spend your time with, rather than waiting to be chosen.

Remember that a poorly written ad will yield poor results. Since your personal ad will be "selling" you, it's imperitive that you make it a winner in order to yield the best results. Study the personals column for ideas. See which ads attract your attention. Then ask yourself what it was about those ads that caught your eye.

There are helpful books on how to write personal ads. One good one is *How to Meet the Opposite Sex Through Personal Ads* by William F. Schopf (Plantation, FL: Fun in the Sun Publications, 1991). Another book is *Personal Ads—Never Be Lonely Again* by Marlene C. Halbig (Laguna Beach, CA: Baron Publications, 1992). Both these books are very thorough in their discussion of how to write, place, and screen ads, and how to respond to them. If you aren't skilled in the area of personal

Decoding the Personals

Half the fun of reading personal ads is trying to decipher the string of abbreviations that starts them off. To help you translate, the following list provides some of the more common abbreviations used in today's publications:

M	Male	W	White
F	Female	B	Black
G	Gay	A	Asian
L	Lesbian	H	Hispanic
BI	Bisexual	J	Jewish
S	Single	C	Christian
D	Divorced	NR	Not religious
WW	Widowed	NS	Nonsmoker
NM	Never married	ISO	In search of

ads, these books (or at least one of them) are a must for you. Nevertheless, following are a few basic pointers regarding the preparation of personal ads:

- When writing a personal ad, be sure to list the basic information about yourself, including age, sex, race, religion, and marital status.

- Include important physical characteristics (height, build, hair color, eye color) and personality qualities (sincerity, honesty, intelligence, sense of humor).

- List any significant "disqualifiers" (physical handicap, smoking) that might eliminate prospects.

- Include any interests and non-negotiables (see page 21) that you will not or cannot compromise on (children, pets, physical fitness activities).

- List what you are seeking in a respondent, including physical characteristics, personality qualities, and non-negotiables, and state what you do not want.

- Keep your ad short. A lengthy ad will not attract more responses. In fact, research has suggested that the opposite may be true. In addition, even though you may want to include every detail about yourself and exactly what you're looking for in a prospect, the more general you keep your ad, the larger the number of respondents will be.

The latest wrinkle in personal ads is twenty-four-hour voice-mail service. You can have a voice-mail box number assigned to your personal ad, so that anybody interested in your ad can phone the voice-mail box number and hear a recorded phone greeting from you. People do like hearing voices. The phone greeting can be just a reading of the newspaper ad, or it can be something completely different and creative. People can also call the publication's special telephone number to browse through many different voice ads. If they find any that interest them, they can punch in the voice-mail box number and leave a message, their name, and their telephone number. The advertisers call in daily or weekly to check their messages.

The wonderful thing about personal ads is that you can advertise for exactly the type of person you would like to meet and may receive a good number of qualified prospects. And you can get all those replies from just one well-written personal ad.

HANDLING RESPONSES TO YOUR AD

When you get responses to your ad, your first step should be to separate the letters sent by those individuals you feel are potentially interesting from the letters of those you have absolutely no wish to meet. Evaluate each letter in terms of how desirable the prospect seems, based on what he or she has written.

You might want to divide your letters into three categories: Category "A" could contain those respondents who seem genuinely interesting, people you intend to contact. Category "C" could contain those people you definitely will not contact. Category "B" could be for those people you are not sure about but haven't yet eliminated; putting them in a "hold" category lets you defer the decision until a later time. Some advertisers never have to turn to category "B," either because they have so many "A" respondents or because they hit it off with somebody in category "A." However, if you have met everyone in your "A" group and have not yet been successful, you can return to the "B" group, re-evaluate the respondents, and follow-up accordingly.

Once you decide who you would like to meet, it's up to you to make the contact. Make your phone conversation simple. Identify yourself by your first name. (If you get an answering machine, *do not* leave your name or telephone number. Why? You may decide that you do not want this person to have your telephone number, so why leave it?) Mention that you had an ad in the personals and give the name of the publication. You can restate the ad, if you would like to, to jog your prospect's memory.

Try to get a light conversation going. You can use lines such as: "Have you ever used the personals before?" or "Do you read the newspaper/magazine often?" or "What type of things do you like to do on a first date?" You should ask very basic questions. Your prospect should not have any trouble holding up the other end of the conversation. If the prospect mentioned something interesting or unusual in his or her letter, ask about it. The more interested you act in your prospect, the more interested your prospect will be in meeting you.

MEETING A PROSPECT

So, now you're having a conversation with your prospect. Do you feel like you want to proceed? Remember, one of the purposes of the initial phone call is to determine if the prospect sounds as interesting in person as in his or her letter. If you feel that the answer is yes, suggest a meeting.

When you arrange to meet somebody, make sure it's on neutral territory. You don't want to invite a stranger to your home, even to just pick you up (and you certainly don't want to go to a stranger's home!), simply because, just as with answering machines, you may decide that you do not want this person to know where you live. By meeting in a busy public place, you'll feel safest, so if it doesn't work out, you won't have to worry about hurting the other person's feelings or about any disappointment expressed by the prospect. Common sites for first meetings are coffee shops and diners. Again, bear in mind that the purpose of this initial meeting is to see if there is any chemistry between you and your prospect.

When you arrange the initial meeting, make sure that each of you knows what the other person looks like or will be wearing. It can be very embarrassing to have to wait for a total stranger to approach you and timidly ask your name, or for you to have to do the same. If you wear something unusual, such as a flower or a cap or a brightly colored scarf, it can make identification much easier and can also be an icebreaker in a situation that many people find awkward.

IF THE PROSPECT DOESN'T WORK OUT

Trust your instincts. You may find that you're uncomfortable with the person you're talking to. Don't try to convince yourself that, because of one particular characteristic, you should disregard your gut feeling. There's nothing wrong with leaving an initial meeting with an open-ended promise such as, "Let me see how I feel," or "Give me some time to think about this, and then we'll talk some more."

Don't feel obligated. Even though your prospect is meeting with you, you are meeting with him or her. If it doesn't seem to be working out, there's no reason to prolong the agony. Simply say, "Thank you very much for meeting with me, but I don't think this would work." As with other lines, practice until you feel confident and comfortable.

If you're not completely sure that you want to meet a prospect again, but you're not ready to strike the person off your list, you may want to set up another "public" meeting. A second meeting may help you to solidify your feelings.

RESPONDING TO AN AD

If you decide to respond to an ad rather than to write your own, remember that the person who placed the ad will probably receive numerous replies. You'll want your reply to stand out. There are a few things you should keep in mind to accomplish this:

- Use colorful paper or even a colorful envelope. This may seem trivial, but it makes your response stand out immediately.

- Make sure that you either use very neat handwriting or type your letter. One of the biggest turnoffs is a sloppily written response.

- Keep your response succinct but include some enticing details.

- Send out freshly typed letters to each ad you respond to.

Another big turnoff is receiving a photocopied response, obviously one of a batch sent out to respond to several ads.

- Make sure that you respond to the wording of the ad rather than just composing a form letter. Even if your letter is freshly typed, if nothing in the letter focuses on the specific ad, it may appear that you're responding to many different ads with the same reply letter. A good response addresses the key words, thoughts, goals, and requested characteristics in the ad.

- Be creative. Nothing works worse than a boring, run-of-the-mill response. Try a unique approach, such as humor—but not too corny, please!

- Sound enthusiastic about meeting the person, but don't sound like you're begging! Sound confident, intelligent, and charming!

If you write an interesting, positive response, you hopefully will soon hear from the placer of the ad. In your telephone conversation, sound natural and sure of yourself, and make certain that you follow the tips given on page 181. Again, try to arrange an initial meeting in a public place and remember that you are not obligated to do anything with anyone you have no interest in.

As with any other technique described in this book, using the personals is a skill, one that you can refine through practice. If you have success right away, great! But if not, don't give up. Learn from your efforts, polish your techniques, and look forward to meeting many more wonderful people.

23. How to Meet Someone During the Holidays

For people who are in relationships or who have families, the holidays can be among the most joyous times of the year. For individuals who are alone, however, the holidays can be depressing and upsetting.

Many singles believe that the worst time of the year to meet prospects is during the holiday season. They feel that everybody is tied up with holiday activities and no one is interested in looking for others. This is far from the truth. How do we know? If it were true, why are so many special events held for singles at this time of year? So, rather than despairing that you have to go through another Thanksgiving, Christmas, Hanukkah, or New Year's Eve alone, let's talk about what you can do to make the most of your holiday season and keep your social life on the upswing.

THINK LOGICALLY

Do you really believe that you are the only single person in town who is both unattached and unoccupied during the holiday season? Of course not. There are many other people out there who are in the same position. Although some of these people may decide to remain at home and just watch holiday specials on television, others will be out trying to increase their social contacts and meet people they can enjoy holiday activities with. (By the way, if holiday specials are a favorite of yours, hook up your VCR, tape the specials, and watch them after you get back from your singles activities!)

But don't procrastinate. Although there are certain times of the year when you can pick yourself up and go out and do things spontaneously with other singles, holiday time is usually not one of them. Many organizations sell tickets to events, but the tickets may sell out quickly. If you wait too long, you may find yourself out in the cold. Warm up to the task and get busy.

WHERE TO MEET PEOPLE DURING THE HOLIDAYS

Many of the contact sites and functions that we have been discussing in Part II of this book will still be applicable at this time of year. Going to dances and parties, as well as dining out, are just as viable at holiday time as they are at any other time of the year. In fact, they may be more appropriate now. Why? Many organizations, restaurants, and clubs sponsor special holiday get-togethers. They recognize, as you should, that there are many eager singles out there who would like to meet others, even at this time of year.

Check with resources that specialize in singles in your quest to meet prospects. Look in the singles sections of your local newspapers. Often, these are the best places to find singles activities listed. Check with organizations that normally sponsor singles activities. Check with restaurants and clubs to see if they have any special events planned for this time of year.

Ask people you know, especially singles, if they're aware of special happenings during the holiday season. "Sure," you might say, "I'll sound desperate, as if I have nothing to do." Well, it really depends on how you ask your questions. If you sound confident and interested, you'll come off fine. On the other hand, if you sound like you're close to tears when you ask, then you may appear desperate.

If you're interested in traveling, check with your local travel agent to find out if any resorts or hotels are sponsoring singles weekends or get-togethers. You can also call hotels and resorts directly. Most facilities have toll-free numbers and will be happy to provide you with any information you request.

GET THE (SNOW)BALL ROLLING

Once you decide to try to meet singles during holiday time, you'll find that you already feel more encouraged and optimistic. It can change your whole frame of mind knowing that instead of having to be home alone, you can go out and meet other people who are also enthusiastically looking to meet singles, pair up, and develop romantic relationships. This is definitely the way to start the new year off on the right foot.

Remember a very important (and clever!) motto: Don't despair, get out there! You're not going to meet anyone sitting at home.

A Bright New Beginning

*I*f you're reading this book, you probably have not had as much success in your social life as you would like. You have decided that you want to learn some additional skills, strategies, or ideas in order to improve your ability to meet people and develop lasting relationships. This book has hopefully brought you some new insight and constructive ideas to help you in your quest for a wonderful relationship.

But now that you've finished reading this book, don't put it away. Don't feel that it must now collect dust on a shelf. Use this book as a resource. Any time you plan on doing anything to meet people, or any time you decide to try a new or different activity, thumb through this book for some helpful hints or suggestions. You may find that each time you go through the book, you pick up a new idea, one you missed during your last review, simply because it did not fit with what you were aiming to accomplish at that particular time.

DON'T LET REJECTION STOP YOU

Remember that in any quest to develop a romantic relationship, rejection is part of the process. If you join a singles activity expecting 100 percent success, you're bound to be disappointed. Do you know any people who have never experienced ups and downs in their quest for the perfect relationship? We don't. Everyone experiences the unpleasantness of rejection.

If you are shot down, you can look at it in a number of different ways. Either you can take it as a personal affront, feel two-feet tall, and decide that you're never going to try to meet someone again! Or you can try to figure out what happened to cause the rejection, so that you can learn from it. Which do you think is the better option?

Rejection should not be a deterrent. In fact, it can strengthen your character, as well as your techniques, so look at the positive side. Any time an attempt does not work out the way you would like, ask yourself what you could have done better—how you could have improved your approach, how you could have delivered your lines better, how you could have presented yourself more confidently, and so on. Practice makes better. Keep practicing your lines, your follow-up conversation, and the way you present yourself. Every bit of knowledge you gain from any experience you have will help you in subsequent attempts.

If you find that you're still having difficulty, watch other people. Look around you, pick out the people who seem to be successful a great portion of the time, and watch carefully what they do. Or ask people how they like to be approached. In the future, you can use everything you learn.

Concerning rejection, there are a lot of reasons that a person may choose not to be interested in you. Keep something in mind: If somebody rejects you, it is not you as a person that is being rejected. Does the prospect really know you from just one preliminary meeting? Of course not. What this person really is rejecting is either something about your presentation or something about your approach.

Do you like everybody you meet? Would you respond favorably to everybody who came up to you? Probably not. So therefore, how can you expect everybody you encounter to respond favorably to you? If someone rejects you, remind yourself that you, too, do not like everybody and then just pull yourself together and move on.

WE'D LIKE TO HEAR FROM YOU

Although we may never meet face to face, we feel that we have interacted with you in the preparation and delivery of this book. We would like to know how our techniques, tips, ideas, and suggestions have worked for you. We would welcome letters from you in which you tell us your success stories. Write to us in care of Avery Publishing Group, 120 Old Broadway, Garden City Park, New York 11040. Tell us what line worked for you. What contact sites did you find most helpful? In addition, let us know what areas you'd like to learn more about. What situations are still difficult for you? Keep us informed. We may be able to use your input in a future publication.

Matter of fact, we just may have provided you with the best icebreaking approach of all. Why not use our request to hear from you as the way to initiate conversations with prospects. You can say something like: "Excuse me. I'm trying to help out someone who is gathering information for a book. The book is on lines and approaches to use for breaking the ice when meeting someone new. Can you help?" (And don't forget to send us the responses!)

It's now time to put what you've learned to good use. Walk tall, be proud, and have fun meeting people. No better cliché can be used for closing this book than to wish you what you wish for yourself!

Index

Activities for singles, how to find, 74–75

Adult education courses, prospecting at, 135–136

Advertisements, personal. *See* Personal advertisements.

Advertisements for singles events, 74–75

Airplanes, and airports, prospecting in, 166–167

Animal rights groups, prospecting at, 96

Animals, as attention getters, 65–66

Antique fairs, prospecting at, 134

Appearance, improving, 6–7

Art galleries, prospecting at, 134–135

Arts and crafts fairs, festivals, and shows, prospecting at, 133–134

Attention getters, 64–69

Attention span, and first impression, 9

Attitude, improving mental, 10–14

Automobiles, prospecting in, 167–170

Automotive stores, prospecting at, 157–158

Barbecues for singles, 104–105

Baseball equipment, as an attention getter, 68

Basketball equipment, as an attention getter, 68

Beaches, prospecting at, 111–113

Bicycling clubs and tours, prospecting at, 115–116

Bike-a-thons, prospecting at, 115–116

Biting nails, and first impression, 9–10

Books, as attention getters, 64

Bookstores, prospecting at, 160–161

Bowling, prospecting while, 127

Breaking the ice, 33–39

Buses, and bus stations, prospecting in, 165–166

Business mixers, seminars, and workshops, prospecting at, 108–109

Button covers, as attention getters, 69

Buttons, as attention getters, 65

Camcorders, as attention getters, 67

Cameras, as attention getters, 67

Camping trips for singles, 114

Camps for singles, 122–123

Card shops, prospecting at, 167–170

Cashiers, as prospects, 162–173

Cat shows, prospecting at, 139–140

Charitable groups, prospecting at, 93–95

Children, as attention getters, 66

Churches, prospecting at, 147–148

Cigarettes, smoking, and first impression, 8

Cigars, smoking, and first impression, 8

Closing techniques
  Extended Close, 49–51
  Quick Close, 47–49
  Semi-Date Close, 51–53
Clothing, and first impression, 7
Clubs
  bicycling, 115–116
  dance, for singles, 78-79
  dining, for singles, 105–106
  jazz, 90–91
  horseback riding, 140-141
  mountain climbing, 117
  single parent, 138
  skydiving, 117
  walking, 116–117
Coffee shops, prospecting at, 100–101
College courses and seminars, prospecting at, 135–136
Community groups, prospecting at, 96–97
Compromising in a relationship, 11–12
Concerts, prospecting at, 88–89
Conventions, prospecting at, 109
Conversation
  follow-up points, 54–55
  skills, 29–30, 31–39
Cracking knuckles, and first impression, 9–10
Cruises for singles, 121–122
Cursing, and first impression, 9–10

Dance clubs, prospecting at, 78–79
Dances
  singles, 77–78
  square, 79–80
Dating services, 173–175
Department stores, prospecting at, 156–157
Diners, prospecting at, 100–101
Dining clubs for singles, 105–106
Dinners for singles, 83–85
Disposition, and first impression, 10–14
Dog shows, prospecting at, 139–140

Dogs, as attention getters, 65–66

Education, adult courses, prospecting at, 135–136
Emotions, expressing, 13
Engagement parties, prospecting at, 85–86
Environmental groups, prospecting at, 95–96
Expressing emotions, 13
Eye contact, and first impression, 9

Fan clubs, prospecting at, 144–145
Farmers markets, prospecting at, 159–160
Fast food restaurants, prospecting at, 101–102
Festivals, music, prospecting at, 88
First impression
  appearance and, 6–7
  attitude and, 10–14, 30
  bad habits and, 8–10
  cursing and, 9–10
  eye contact and, 9
  knuckle cracking and, 9–10
  manners and, 7–8
  nail biting and, 9–10
  smoking and, 8
  staring and, 9
  yawning and, 9
Fitness centers, prospecting at, 141–142
Flea markets, prospecting at, 158
Flexibility. *See* Compromising in a relationship.
Follow-up conversation points, 54–55
Foul language, and first impression, 9–10
Fun eateries, prospecting at, 102

Gambling junkets for singles, 123–124
Game nights for singles, 87–88
Get-aways, singles weekends, 119–120
Golf-outings for singles, 129–130

Gyms, prospecting at, 141

Habits, bad, eliminating, 8–10
Hairstyles, as attention getters, 68
Hats, as attention getters, 66
Hayrides for singles, 114–115
Headbands, as attention getters, 66–67
Health food stores, prospecting at, 155
Holidays, prospecting during, 186–187
Honesty, expressing, 13
Horseback riding clubs, prospecting at, 140–141
Horse shows, prospecting at, 139–140
Hot buttons, 16
House parties for singles, 82
Houses of worship, prospecting at, 147–148
Humor, when to use, 60–62
Humor Technique, Use-of-, 60–62

Icebreaking lines, 33–39
Impression, first. *See* First impression.
Industry mixers, seminars, and workshops, prospecting at, 108–109

Jazz clubs, prospecting at, 90–91
Jokes, when to use, 60–62

Karaoke sing-a-longs, prospecting at, 91–92
Kids, as attention getters, 66
Kites, as attention getters, 68
Knuckle cracking, and first impression, 9–10

Laid-Back Technique, 59
Language, foul, and first impression, 9–10
Laundromats, prospecting at, 148–150
Lectures, prospecting at, 136–137
Libraries, prospecting at, 150

Lines, prospecting while waiting on, 151–152
Lines for
adult education courses, 136
airplanes and airports, 167
animal rights groups, 96
antique fairs, 134
art galleries, 135
arts and crafts fairs, 134
automobiles, 170
automotive stores, 157–158
barbecues, 105
beaches, 112–113
bicycling clubs and tours, 116
bike-a-thons, 116
bookstores, 161
bowling, 127
breaking the ice, 33–39
buses and bus stations, 166
camping trips, 114
camps, 123
card shops, 160
cars, 170
cashiers, 162
charitable groups, 95
churches, 148
coffee shops, 101
college courses, 136
community groups, 97
conventions, 109
cruises, 122
dance clubs, 79
dances, 78
department stores, 156–157
diners, 101
dining clubs, 106
dinners, 84–85
driving, 170
engagement parties, 86
environmental groups, 96
fan clubs, 144–145
farmers markets, 159–169
fast food restaurants, 102
fitness centers, 142
flea markets, 158

follow-up, 42–43, 44, 45
fun eateries, 102
gambling junkets, 124
game nights, 88
golfing, 129–130
gyms, 142
hay rides, 115
health food stores, 155
horseback riding clubs, 141
house parties, 82
house sales, 159
houses of worship, 148
industry mixers, seminars, and
   workshops, 108
jazz clubs, 91
Karaoke sing-a-longs, 92
laundromats, 149–150
lectures, 137
libraries, 150
long lines, 151–152
luncheons, 84–85
malls, 156
mixers, 108
movie theaters, 90
museums, 135
music festivals, 89
parks, 113–114
parties, 81–82
part-time jobs, 110
picnics, 105
pizza parlors, 100
political groups, 98
pool parties, 83
pools, 112–113
PTA meetings, 138
record stores, 161
retreats, 124
salad bars, 103
school meetings, 138
seminars, 108
shopping malls, 156
single parent clubs, 138
skiing, 129
softball games, 126
specialty restaurants, 103

sporting events, 130
sports bars, 130
square dances, 79–80
supermarkets, 154
swap meets, 158
synagogues, 148
tennis outings, 128
tours, 121
trade shows, 109
traffic jams, 171
trains and train stations, 166
transcendental meditation (TM)
   classes, 142–143
vacations, 120–121
video stores, 162
volleyball games, 126–127
waiting rooms, 151
walking clubs, 116–117
walleyball games, 126–127
weddings, 86
weekend get-aways, 120
workshops, 108
yard sales, 159
yoga classes, 142–143
Lists of prospects, forming, 15–21
Love Connection, 175
Luncheons for singles, 83–85

Magazines, as attention getters, 64
Malls, prospecting at, 155–156
Manners, and first impression, 7–8
Meditation, classes, prospecting at,
   142
Meeting a prospect, 182
Movie theaters, prospecting at, 134
Museums, prospecting at, 134
Music festivals, prospecting at, 88–89

Nail biting, and first impression, 9–10
Negative attitude, 11
Networking, 24–25

Organizations
   animal rights, 96
   charitable, 93–95

community, 96–97
environmental, 95–96
political, 97–98

Parent clubs, single, prospecting at, 138
Parks, prospecting at, 113–114
Parties for singles, 80–83
Part-time jobs, prospecting at, 110
Personal advertisements
responding to, 183–184
responses from, handling, 180–181
writing, 178–180
Personality, improving, 11
Pets, as attention getters, 65–66
Physical appearance, improving, 6–7
Picnics for singles, 104–105
Pipes, smoking, and first impression, 8
Pizza parlors, prospecting at, 99–100
Political groups and parties, prospecting at, 97–98
Pool parties for singles, 82–83
Pools, prospecting at, 111–113
Positive attitude, 10–14
Preparation, importance of, 26–27
Prospects
developing a list of, 15–21
rejection by, 13–14, 43, 44–45, 58, 190–191
rejection of, 182–183
PTA meetings, prospecting at, 137–138
Put-downs, self, 60–61

Quick-Close technique, 47–49

Record stores, prospecting at, 160–161
Rejection
by prospects, 13–14, 43, 44–45, 58, 190–191
of prospects, 182–183
Requirements for prospects, 21–22
Responses, handling, 42–45

Restaurants, prospecting at, 99–103
Retreats, prospecting at, 124

Salad bars, prospecting at, 103–104
School meetings, prospecting at, 137–138
Seed-Planting technique, 57–59
Semi-Date Close technique, 51–53
Shopping malls, prospecting at, 155–156
Signs, as attention getters, 64–65
Sing-a-longs, karaoke, prospecting at, 91–92
Singles events
barbecues, 104–105
bowling leagues, 127
camping trips, 114
camps 122–123
cruises, 121–122
dances, 77–78
dining clubs, 105–106
dinners, 83–85
gambling junkets, 123–124
game nights, 87–88
golf outings, 129–130
hay rides, 114–115
how to find, 74–75
luncheons, 83–85
parent clubs, 138
parties, 80–83
picnics, 104–105
ski weekends, 128–129
square dances, 79–80
tennis outings, 128
tours, 121
Skiing weekends for singles, 128–129
Smoking, and first impression, 8
Socks, as attention getters, 67-68
Softball games, prospecting at, 125–126
Specialty restaurants, prospecting at, 103
Sports bars, prospecting at, 130–131
Sports equipment, as an attention getter, 68

Sporting events, prospecting at, 125–130

Square dances, prospecting at, 79–80

Staring, and first impression, 9

Supermarkets, prospecting at, 153–154

Support groups, prospecting at, 143–144

Swap meets, prospecting at, 158

Synagogues, prospecting at, 148

Table manners, and first impression, 8

Techniques
 Extended-Close, 47–49
 Laid-Back, 59
 Quick-Close, 47–49
 Seed-Planting, 57–59
 Semi-Date Close, 51–53
 Use-of-Humor, 60–62

Tee shirts, as attention getters, 65

Tennis equipment, as an attention getter, 68

Tennis outings for singles, 128

Ties, as attention getters, 67–68

Tours, bicycling, prospecting at, 115–116

Trade shows, prospecting at, 109

Traffic jams, prospecting in, 170–171

Trains and train stations, prospecting in, 165–166

Transcendental meditation (TM) classes, prospecting at, 142

Travel brochures, as attention getters, 67

Use-of-Humor technique, 60–62

Vacation brochures, as attention getters, 67

Video stores, prospecting at, 161–162

Volleyball
 equipment, as an attention getter, 68
 games, prospecting at, 126–127

Waiting rooms, prospecting in, 150–151

Walk-a-thons and walkfests, prospecting at, 116–117

Walking clubs, prospecting at, 116–117

Walleyball games, prospecting at, 126–127

Weddings, prospecting at, 85–86

Weekend get-aways for singles, 119–120

Willpower, 12

Workshops, adult education, prospecting at, 135–136

Worship, houses of, prospecting at, 147–148

Yard sales, prospecting at, 159

Yawning, and first impression, 9

Yoga classes, prospecting at, 142–143

Other Interesting Books From Avery

LOVE TACTICS

How to Win the One You Want
Thomas McKnight and Robert H. Phillips

Is there anything you can do to make that special someone want you as much as you want them? Absolutely! With *Love Tactics*, you will learn the most effective ways of developing meaningful relationships, intimacy, and—ultimately—love.

Whether you're very shy, a little on the quiet side, or simply not the social success you'd like to be, *Love Tactics* is the perfect self-help guide to romantic success. This classic title has sold over 100,000 copies. Personal relations consultant Thomas W. McKnight and practicing psychologist Robert H. Phillips effectively explain how you can build self-confidence, gain trust, and keep that special someone interested and hoping for a true commitment.

For the 70 million single people in America who are searching for the love of their life, this practical manual may even make loneliness a thing of the past. **$7.95**

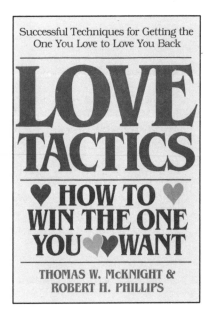

Successful Techniques for Getting the One You Love to Love You Back

LOVE TACTICS
♥ HOW TO ♥ WIN THE ONE YOU ♥♥ WANT

THOMAS W. McKNIGHT & ROBERT H. PHILLIPS

MORE LOVE TACTICS

How to Win That Special Someone
Thomas McKnight and Robert H. Phillips

More Love Tactics picks up where the best-seller *Love Tactics* leaves off, providing a host of new and effective strategies to help you win the one you want, and in addition, addressing many important areas not covered in the first book.

Each of the four parts of *More Love Tactics* contains practical ways to reach your goal. Part One focuses on being the person you want—getting yourself ready to meet that special someone. Part Two tells you how to find the one you want—where to look, what to join, and how to make that crucial first contact. Part Three centers on winning the one you want—learning the tactics needed to get the one you like to like you back. And Part Four tells you how to win back the one you've lost. In this section, you'll find terrific ways to rekindle, revive, or retrieve that special past romance.

More Love Tactics can provide you with that all-important psychological edge you need to tip the scales in your favor. **$8.95**

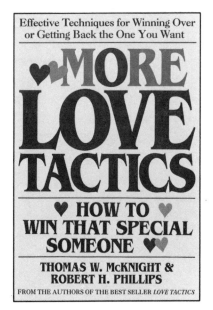

Effective Techniques for Winning Over or Getting Back the One You Want

MORE LOVE TACTICS
♥ HOW TO ♥ WIN THAT SPECIAL SOMEONE ♥♥

THOMAS W. McKNIGHT & ROBERT H. PHILLIPS
FROM THE AUTHORS OF THE BEST SELLER *LOVE TACTICS*

Available at Your Local Bookseller.
For a Complete Catalog of Our Books, Call Us at 1-800-548-5757.

Singles Survival Times newsletter is for the single-minded single. It features unique methods for meeting prospects, tried and new icebreaking lines, nutrition and health tips, recipes for one, and information on free personal ads. To receive three complimentary issues of *Singles Survival Times* newsletter, complete the form below and mail it to:

Singles Survival Times
P.O. Box 1332
Bensalem, PA 19020

— — — — — — — — — — — — — — — — — — — —

Please print:

Name _____

Address _____

City _____

State _____ Zip _____

Note: Singles Survival Times newsletter is neither affiliated with nor published by Avery Publishing Group.